Circle of Giving

Circle of
Giving

---

by *Ellen Howard*

ATHENEUM

New York

The author thanks Tom Burnam and Zola Helen Ross
for their help and encouragement.

LIBRARY OF CONGRESS CATALOGING IN PUBLICATION DATA

Howard, Ellen.   The circle of giving.

SUMMARY: *When twelve-year-old Marguerite moves to Los
Angeles in the late 1920s, she suddenly becomes shy,
withdrawn, and ill at ease with other children until
a girl with cerebral palsy moves in across the street.
[1. Moving, Household—Fiction.   2. Cerebral palsy
—Fiction.   3. Physically handicapped—Fiction]   I. Title.
PZ7.H83274Ci   1984   [Fic]   83-15631*
ISBN 0-689-31027-7

Atheneum
Macmillan Publishing Company
866 Third Avenue, New York, NY 10022
Collier Macmillan Canada, Inc.

Composition by Service Typesetters, Austin, Texas
Printed and bound by Fairfield Graphics,
Fairfield, Pennsylvania
Designed by Mary Ahern

5 7 9 11 13 15 17 19 F/C 20 18 16 14 12 10 8 6

For Betty Jeane and Daisidel—and Betsie

Contents

1 • *The House Across the Street* 3

2 • *The Piano* 9

3 • *The Hanisians* 12

4 • *Francie* 18

5 • *My Sister, Marguerite* 22

6 • *A Real Little Girl* 25

7 • *Friends with Francie* 31

8 • *Teaching Francie* 37

9 • *California Autumn* 41

10 • *The Championship* 46

11 • *Real Words* 54

12 • *Marguerite's Idea* 58

13 • *Everybody for Christmas* 64

14 • *Just Like Us* 69

15 • *The Party* 76

16 • *Francie and the Kids* 82

17 • *The Gift* 87

18 • *Circle of Giving* 94

Circle of Giving

1

The House Across the Street

THE SUMMER before my tenth birthday, our family moved to California because, "It's the land of opportunity," Daddy said. "There are jobs," said Mother.

"I thought California would be glamorous," said my sister, Marguerite. "I thought there'd be movie stars and stuff." But the closest thing our neighborhood had to a movie star was Mr. Dooley, who was a bookkeeper at Metro-Goldwyn-Mayer. No one glamorous came to live on Stanley Avenue . . . until the Hanisians moved into the house across the street.

Because our family was among the first to move into the brand new houses on Stanley Avenue, we were able to watch as each of the other houses was sold and each new family moved in. Keeping track of new neighbors became a sort of self-appointed duty for Marguerite and me. Finally, there was only one empty house left—the house across the street.

Every Sunday, the real estate man would show the house across the street to chattering ladies in feathered hats and gentlemen who looked bored. Sometimes he would sit at a card table just inside the door and play solitaire and no one would come to see the house all day. At dusk he would fold up the table and prop it against the wall with the chair beside it. Then he would lock the door and go away again for another week.

"I wonder why that house doesn't sell," our mother would say. "It's just like all the rest."

"Maybe it's waiting for someone," Daddy said.

Later, Marguerite and I agreed he was right. The house across the street was waiting for the Hanisians.

FROM the very first day, we were irresistibly drawn to the Hanisians.

A large van turned onto our street right after breakfast one Saturday morning late in the spring. I was sitting on the front steps, picking a scab on my knee and waiting for someone to come out to play. I could hear the Dooley baby crying from the far end of the block, and Mrs. Lord, shrill over the whir of Mr. Lord's lawn mower, hollering from her porch. Through an open window, Mrs. Sisson's piano rang forth with Sammy Benjamin's laborious, but loud, rendering of "Flow Gently, Sweet Afton."

The van stopped, and I was on my feet in an instant. Something interesting was going to happen today. Someone was moving into the house across the street!

"Marguerite," I yelled, running into the house. "Marguerite, come and see. The new people across the street are here!"

Marguerite had been spending a lot of time fooling with her hair ever since she turned twelve in January. I had a pretty good idea where to find her, and sure enough, she was at our dressing table, mooning into the mirror, when I ran into our room that morning. But at my news, she jumped right up and came out to join me on the steps.

We watched, squinting against the morning sun, as the moving men, clad in overalls, let down the ramp on the back of the van and opened the big doors. We could not see inside, but we could imagine what was there—chairs and tables and a sofa and beds and boxes, piles and piles of boxes!

Marguerite and I had gotten expert at guessing the size and character of a new family, just from their belongings. "Kids," Marguerite would say if a box of toys was carried in, or "A baby," if we saw a high chair or a crib. "They like to read," I would announce if I saw the moving men strain under heavy boxes of books. It was me who guessed Mrs. Lord was a good cook, just from the number and variety of her pots and pans, before we even saw how plump the whole family was.

But this morning, the moving men seemed to take forever to begin unloading our new neighbors' things. Marguerite and I could hear them grunting and heaving at something heavy in the back of the van. There were thumps and scufflings, and the van swayed a little with the activity inside it.

"Maybe they've got a pet elephant," I said, trying to make a joke, but Marguerite acted as if she hadn't heard me. She was gazing down the street toward Mrs. Sisson's house, her head cocked to hear the music that floated from the window. Mrs. Sisson must be playing now, I thought, because Sammy sure wasn't that good. I looked up and down Stanley Avenue, feeling bored and a little sad.

All the houses on Stanley Avenue looked alike. They were new and shiny white, with red tile roofs. The real estate man had called them "Spanish bungalows," and Marguerite and I had thought that sounded terribly romantic. "But it's not," said Marguerite when we first saw our new house. "It's not romantic at all, Jeannie. It's *ordinary* and just like all the rest."

Our house sat on its own little square of new green lawn, as all the houses did. A row of scraggly palm trees marched along the parking strip in front, and the sidewalk ran between the lawns and parkings like a smooth gray ribbon. "Great for skating, I bet," I told Marguerite, trying to cheer her up when we first saw it. I patted my skate key, hanging from a string around my neck.

It was good for skating, we soon found out—smooth and bumpless—but that didn't cheer Marguerite. "Not a crack in it," she would shout as we whizzed along, side by side, holding hands. "It's dull!" she would say. "Just like the houses, just like the people, just like us!" And her arm would wave about in despair, pointing out the square white houses, the thin green lawns, the straight rows of skinny palms, until she unbalanced us and sent me, arms flailing, shooting off the walk to fall in a heap on the grass.

She was right, in a way. The houses were ordinary and all alike, and until the Hanisians came, we and our neighbors seemed ordinary and very nearly alike as well.

All of the families who moved to Stanley Avenue had mothers who kept house and fathers who went to work each day. "That's what brought us here, after all," said Mother. "Work—at the studios or the airplane factories or the oil plants at Long Beach." Like our mother, the mothers wore aprons over flowered house dresses. The fathers wore navy blue suits and clean white shirts or blue work shirts and heavy laced-up boots.

Most of the families had children. The Dooleys on the corner had the most, six in all, from Alexander who, at fourteen, was the oldest kid on the block, to the baby, Gerald, who sucked his thumb. "I don't know where they put them all, in that little house," said our mother, clucking her tongue. But if Marguerite and I had been asked who was most interesting on Stanley Avenue—before the Hanisians moved in—we would have said the Dooleys. "At least there's usually something *happening* at the Dooleys," Marguerite said.

"At home," said Marguerite with a faraway look in her eye, and I knew she meant our little town in Oregon, "at home, there were grandparents . . . and bachelors . . . and, and widows. On Stanley Avenue, there are only mothers and fathers and kids, like us." Her voice was cranky, and there was an ugly, discontented pucker to Marguerite's face when she said things like that. She didn't seem like the Marguerite I had always loved. But then, she had been acting funny ever since we moved—quiet and unhappy, and sometimes even mad. I knew she hadn't wanted to move; but then, neither had I—and *I* hadn't changed. Sometimes, I even wondered if Marguerite felt shy among our new neighbors, but that was hard to believe. After all, I thought, Marguerite was everything anyone could ever want to be—pretty and smart and talented. . . . How could a person like Marguerite feel shy?

Still, she sure wasn't like she used to be—easy to talk to and fun to be with. After more than half a year, she hadn't made any friends, and more and more, she seemed to go away even from me to a place inside herself. It made my throat ache to see her sitting beside me, unaware I was there. She nodded her head to the music and moved her fingers on her knee, pretending to play on imaginary piano keys, and I wished something would happen to make her talk to me. I glanced up hopefully when I heard a screen door slam, but it was only Mr. Mendenhall next door, coming out to work in his yard.

Marguerite swayed, lost in the music, her arms hugged around her drawn-up knees.

2

The Piano

"LOOK, MARGUERITE," I cried suddenly, yanked from my thoughts by the object that was at last being hoisted out of the van.

It was a piano—a piano such as we had never seen before. Massive and gleaming, it was so large we knew it would fill the tiny living room of the house across the street. "There'll be no room for the furniture," I whispered, my eyes wide. But once again Marguerite didn't answer me. She just stared and stared, her breath held, the piano mirrored in her shining eyes.

I knew what she was thinking. If there was anything in the world Marguerite wanted, it was a piano. I had seen that same dreaming look in her eyes when she fingered the keys of the Lord girls' piano and when she listened to piano music on the phonograph. Every time we walked past the music store downtown, we would stop in front of the window and look in with envy and longing at the solidly scrolled upright pianos.

"Pianos just cost too much," Marguerite would say,

her lower lip pouting the way it did when she was angry. "I'll never get to play the piano, Jeannie. Never. Never. Never!"

All the kids on Stanley Avenue took music lessons. Well brought up children were expected to be musical in the late 1920s. It was like having good manners and passing grades. Louise Dooley played the accordian, and her sister, Alice Jane, labored over the clarinet. Marguerite and I took tap dancing. Even Warren Mendenhall, the neighborhood bookworm, was forced to practice the tuba half an hour every day. But the Lord girls and Lloyd Timothy and Sammy Benjamin were the lucky ones. Every Saturday morning they got to march proudly down the street to Mrs. Sisson's house, one at a time, for piano lessons.

"Why can't we take piano," I whined sometimes to Mother. Marguerite didn't even ask. We both knew the answer. It was because the Timothys and the Lords and the Benjamins had pianos to practice on, and we did not.

When scales and duets and "easy pieces" filled the Saturday morning air, there'd be a sad, hurting sound to Marguerite's voice. "I could do better than that," she would say. "I know I could."

But the piano being carried into the house across the street was nothing like our neighbors' pianos. It was like nothing real we'd ever seen. It was a piano from the movies or magazine pictures. It was, our mother told us later, a concert grand. And the delicately carved music stand, the elegant curve of its lifted cover, instantly won our allegiance from the sturdy uprights we had formerly admired.

The piano was our first hint that our new neighbors were going to be interesting. We couldn't know how interesting! We couldn't know about Mrs. Hanisian and her pretty teen-aged daughters and the glamorous life they had led. And of course, we never even dreamed of Francie. . . .

Until that day, each red tile roof on Stanley Avenue seemed to cover a family much like us—ordinary and all alike, Marguerite had said.

"How come we thought that?" I asked her later. "How come we didn't think about the funny way Mr. and Mrs. Mendenhall talk, or Mrs. Lord's drawl, for that matter? How come we never noticed Sammy goes to church on Friday evenings, or heard that Lloyd's relatives live in England?"

"Maybe," said Marguerite, "maybe because, until the Hanisians came, we all *looked* pretty much alike. I dunno. I guess I was so busy thinking about myself, I didn't stop to wonder about the neighbors. I thought all families were just about the same. . . ."

But that began to change the moment we first saw the piano. And then we saw Mrs. Hanisian herself step out of a taxi that had stopped in front of the house across the street.

3

The Hanisians

THE LADY who got out of the taxi looked very different from the mothers on Stanley Avenue. That she was a mother was perfectly clear, because with her were two girls, slender older girls with olive skins and shining dark hair and deep-set, dark-fringed eyes. They were fashionably dressed in jumper blouses and short swingy skirts and bandeaus tied low across their foreheads.

"Very ritzy," I said.

But Marguerite wasn't looking at the girls. She was looking at the lady, Mrs. Hanisian, as we came to know.

Mrs. Hanisian was more beautiful than her daughters, beautiful in the way movie stars were beautiful. Her hair was raven black and pulled smoothly away from her face into a shining coil at the nape of her neck, which somehow on her looked elegant instead of old-fashioned. Her face was carefully made up, her high cheekbones rouged, her brows plucked thin and arched high. A soft cloche hat was pulled low over her eyes, its jet black plume sweeping against her cheek. Her black crepe dress, slender and low-waisted and pinned with a glittering brooch, and her high-heeled shoes were far finer than even Mother's best, the outfit she saved for dinner parties and going out with Daddy.

"Glamorous," Marguerite breathed.

A LOT OF TALK—"Gossip," Mother said, sniffing—accompanied the arrival of the Hanisians in our neighborhood.

"Sure, and it's mighty fancy get-ups for *our* part of town," said Mrs. Dooley.

"Perhaps she is a seamstress," Mother said.

"Could be," said Mrs. Timothy, over the fence. "Lots of them foreigners is tailors and such. They must be foreigners with that peculiar name. I can't even say it. And have you seen the girls? They look foreign, right enough."

"Or there's a touch of the tarbrush in the family," drawled Mrs. Lord. "Down home in Lou'siana, we'd have a pretty good idea where skins *that* dark came from."

"Where *is* Mr. Hanisian, now you mention it?" said Mrs. Dooley.

I wondered that myself. "Where's the father?" I whispered to Marguerite that first morning.

"Perhaps . . ." said Marguerite, dreamily, "perhaps he's passed away. Perhaps she is a widow. The Merry Widow. . . ."

I could see Marguerite liked the idea. "There's nothing merry about her," I said in disgust. "You make her sound like Santa Claus."

The truth was far more shocking, but we did not learn it until much later, and even then nobody told us.

Mrs. Hanisian's story came to us bit by bit, overheard from grown-ups' talk, and part of it Mrs. Hanisian told us herself. She had been the daughter of a wealthy cattle baron. "A real heiress," Mother said, "and beautiful and talented too." But her father disowned her when she eloped with Mr. Hanisian, an obscure Armenian composer. "Pay no attention to gossip, girls," Mother said once. "The Hanisian girls got their lovely olive skin and beautiful eyes from their father. Armenians are often dark-complected."

"Armenian." Marguerite would roll the word on her tongue, savoring the exotic sound of it. "Armenian."

"Why 'poor starving Armenians'?" I asked, remembering how Mother sometimes urged Marguerite to eat by telling her Armenian children would be grateful for the amount she left on her plate. Mother explained how the Turks had killed and starved Armenians in their homeland far away at about the time Marguerite was born. "Mr. Hanisian left Armenia before it got so very bad," Mother said. "He was fortunate."

"It was Mr. Hanisian who introduced me to Caruso," Mrs. Hanisian said. And it was Mr. Caruso who had helped launch her career as a concert pianist.

We could scarcely believe anyone we knew had actually known the legendary opera singer, the great Enrico Caruso himself.

"Did you ever talk to him?" I remember asking her, trying to grasp the fact he had been a real person.

"Often," she replied.

I tried to take this in. "Did you *touch* him?" I gasped. Mrs. Hanisian looked startled—then laughed.

It made no sense to me that Mrs. Hanisian's father had disowned her, not when her marriage had brought her into such exalted company!

Mr. and Mrs. Hanisian traveled all over the world on Mrs. Hanisian's concert tours. "Marie was born in Vienna," Mrs. Hanisian said. We looked at Marie, the oldest Hanisian girl, in awe. "Zadora was born in Copenhagen." We weren't certain where that was, but it sounded romantic. "And Francie was born in London."

"They have excellent doctors in London, I've heard," Mother said. "It's a wonder they couldn't do something for Francie."

Francie was Mrs. Hanisian's littlest girl, and by then we knew all about her. But the first day, the day the moving van and the taxi came, only Marie and Zadora were with Mrs. Hanisian, and it did not occur to us there might be another child.

"Where's the father," I had asked Marguerite in a whisper.

It was not until I overheard Mother and Daddy talking, months later, I knew for sure.

"Taking Francie all over the world, looking for a doctor who could cure her, must have cost a fortune," I heard

Mother say. "Perhaps it was the financial strain, or the fact she is so obsessive about the child. . . ."

"That's as may be," Daddy said, "but there's no excuse for a man deserting his family." And so, at last, I understood Mrs. Hanisian was divorced.

"Just like a movie star," said Marguerite, and I could see she was intrigued. We had never known a divorcée before.

Marguerite and I used to wonder what brought the extraordinary Hanisians to, of all places, our neighborhood. The other families had come to California because the fathers needed work.

"But Mrs. Hanisian was famous," Marguerite would say.

"And rich," I would add.

"Maybe she's in hiding—too proud to take her father's help in her time of trial, since he cut her off without a penny when she married," guessed Marguerite.

Later, when they had become friends, I heard Mrs. Hanisian give Mother a different explanation.

"It is quiet here," I heard her say, gazing into the steaming amber of her cup of tea. "Quiet and ordinary and . . . anonymous. Here we can live peacefully, without the stares and whispers. Here people will get used to Francie in time. They will cease being curious. Eventually they will not think of us at all. . . ."

"But your music," Mother said. "It seems such a shame to waste your God-given talent."

Mrs. Hanisian looked at my mother. I sat as still as

I could, knowing both had forgotten I was there. I saw the darkness in Mrs. Hanisian's blue eyes, and I will never forget the twisting bitterness of her voice.

"God gave me Francie also," she said. "Perhaps because I was so proud. Performing was everything to me . . . everything. To walk across a stage and hear the applause, to play and make the audience weep, or laugh or spring to their feet crying 'Brava!' I thought it entitled me to selfishness, to adulation, to love. And then Francie was given me . . ." Her voice dropped so low, I am not sure I heard, but I think she said, ". . . for punishment."

"Oh, my dear!" said Mother, but Mrs. Hanisian got up abruptly, gathered up the tea things, and carried them away to the kitchen, and Mother sat, biting her lip and twisting her handkerchief in her hands.

When Mrs. Hanisian came back, the dark look was gone from her eyes and her voice sounded matter-of-fact. She began to talk of everyday things, and I never heard her speak that way again, nor did Mother ever mention it, so far as I know, so that sometimes I wonder if I imagined the whole thing.

Whatever the reasons for it, Mrs. Hanisian's presence among us brought just what Marguerite had been longing for—glamour and excitement. We adored Mrs. Hanisian for her beauty and tragedy. We admired Marie and Zadora for their age and mystery—they were in high school. But in the end, it was Francie we loved, though no one was more surprised by the fact than Marguerite and me.

4

Francie

OTHER THAN Helen Keller, the famous deaf/blind lady our mother saw once on a lecture tour, Marguerite and I had never known of a handicapped person firsthand before we met Francie.

The neighbors called her "the little paralyzed girl."

"Poor little paralyzed girl," we heard Mrs. Mendenhall tell Mother. "Vat a trial for the mother."

"She ought to be in an institution," said Mrs. Timothy. "My Lloyd gets real upset ev'ry time he sees her."

"Could you put her away, if she were yours?" our mother said. "We should thank our lucky stars we are blessed with healthy children!"

Now I know Francie was not really paralyzed at all. She had cerebral palsy, which means she could not control her muscles because, before she was born, her brain had been hurt somehow. But at first we did not think about what was wrong with Francie. At first, we did not even think about the fact she was handicapped. To us, Francie was simply, horribly, fascinatingly *different* from everyone we knew.

It was the next Saturday after the Hanisians moved onto our street that we first saw Francie scooting down the sidewalk in front of her house in a walker someone had made for her—an old bicycle seat in a frame with wheels. She was strapped to the seat and supported by the frame. Her pitifully thin legs propelled her along the walk with jerking kicks at the pavement. Her great head, much too large for her body, lolled to one side on a spindly neck. Her arms and legs were in constant, spastic motion.

We stood, Marguerite and I, clutching each other by the hand, and stared until our mother called us in.

"I'm ashamed of you," she said. "I never dreamed *my* girls could be so rude—just standing there gawking at that poor unfortunate child. How would *you* feel if you were she? To have other children stare at you like a monkey in the zoo?"

How would *we* feel? It had not occurred to me the creature could feel at all. Was she then like me inside, even though on the outside she was so dreadfully different? Mother assured us she was. I remained privately doubtful, but I didn't say so. I wished Mother would finish her lecture, so we could go play and forget the peculiar little girl.

But Marguerite would not stop talking about her. What was wrong with her, she wanted to know. How long had she been like that? Could she walk? Could she talk?

What did it feel like to be crippled?

"I don't know much about her, Marguerite," Mother said, and I shifted my weight impatiently from foot to foot. "I hear she was born afflicted," said Mother. "It may be she isn't bright. Some unfortunate people have brains that work very slowly. They cannot think or understand as normal people do. But all people, crippled or whole, feeble-minded or intelligent, have the same emotions. We all feel hurt or happiness, no matter the condition of our brains or bodies. That's why it is important to be kind."

I sighed.

Marguerite nodded thoughtfully, absorbed in Mother's explanation.

I squirmed, eager to get away.

Marguerite and Mother paid no attention to me.

"Why not try to get to know her," Mother suggested. Her voice was gentle, and she looked hard at Marguerite. "That poor little girl is going to have an even harder time than you making friends in a new neighborhood. I imagine she would love to have someone to play with."

Marguerite nodded again, and there was a funny look on her face—a little, I thought, as though she felt like crying.

It had been decided. Marguerite and I were to be Francie Hanisian's friends. I was not enthusiastic. But for some reason, Marguerite was determined, and if Marguerite was going to do something in those days, I didn't want to be left behind. Besides, I *was* intrigued by Francie.

Looking at her gave me a squirmy feeling, like looking at the two-headed snake at the county fair. I wouldn't mind seeing her a little closer up. It would be something to tell the other kids.

Mother never did waste time, once a thing was decided. She went straight to the telephone and rang up Mrs. Hanisian. "The girls will be over after lunch," I heard her say. "Not at all. They're anxious to make her welcome in the neighborhood."

Marguerite and I kept looking at each other over our peanut butter sandwiches. I could tell Marguerite was nervous. She only nibbled at her lunch, and I ended up having to eat half her sandwich when Mother wasn't looking and to drink practically all her milk. I was stuffed by the time Mother said we could be excused.

Mother made me change my stockings, because the ones I had on were grass-stained, and Marguerite said she had to comb her hair again, but at last we were walking up the Hanisian's front walk. Marguerite suddenly hesitated on the top step. She pulled back the hand she had reached out to ring the bell and looked at me uncertainly.

"Go on," I hissed. "This was your big idea!"—which wasn't fair. It had, after all, been Mother's idea, and I had not objected out loud. But I was in no mood to be charitable. Having come this far, I figured there was no going back. "What'sa matter?" I jeered. "Afraid?"

Marguerite squared her shoulders and rang the bell.

5

My Sister, Marguerite

MY SISTER, Marguerite, was the prettiest, smartest, most popular girl in our town in Oregon. From the time we were little, I can remember Mother's lady-friends saying, "Marguerite is simply the loveliest child!" "What beautiful blonde hair." "Such a delicate complexion." "A perfect little lady!"

About me they said, "Jeannie is so wholesome!" "The picture of health." "She looks like her father, don't you think?" and "She's a nice little girl." It used to make me mad sometimes, the way Marguerite was petted and praised, but I had to admit it was the truth. Marguerite was beautiful and wonderful. I was just an ordinary kid.

Most everything was easy for Marguerite. She seemed to get A's without half trying. Marguerite taught herself how to read when she was four, and she was artistic and musical and good at hand writing and recitation.

I learned to read in first grade out of the good old *Elson Reader*, just like everybody else. I couldn't even stay inside the lines of a coloring book or carry a tune in a bucket. And my handwriting still looks babyish, and I stutter when I recite.

In Oregon, all the kids followed Marguerite around, wanting to play with her at recess or sit with her at lunch or invite her over after school. Of course I had friends of my own—my best friend, Phyllis Reilly, and some other kids I liked to play with—but lots of times I just tagged along with Marguerite and her friends. And most of the time, that was fine with her.

I loved to be with Marguerite. She could always think of fun things to do. She could make up pretend games like "wild horses," and "Indian princesses," and in the summer time, "bathing beauties." And at night, Marguerite used to tell me stories in bed. I was proud Marguerite was my sister. I loved to look at her and listen to her and be near the kind of magic she seemed to radiate. She was exciting! I guess that's it. There was a special excitement in anything that had to do with Marguerite.

At least that's the way it was in Oregon.

In California, on Stanley Avenue, something strange happened to Marguerite. Of course she was still pretty and smart, but for some reason, no one in our new school or our new neighborhood seemed to notice how special she was. At school, the teachers treated her just like every other kid, and as for the girls in her class, they circled like bees to honey around a stuck-up girl named Shirley Snider. Oh, they were nice enough to Marguerite—as nice to her as they were to me, I guess—but it wasn't like in

Oregon where everyone waited to see what Marguerite would do or say before they decided for themselves.

And Marguerite was different, too. Where she had been vivacious and talkative, she got serious and quiet. She acted as if she couldn't think of anything to say—not friendly at all. She blushed and cried at every little thing, and her stomach was upset a lot, and she began to get pale and thin.

Mother worried about her nerves. "I don't think this climate is good for Marguerite's nerves," she said to Daddy. "The child seems to be going to pieces."

"She's having a rough time settling in," Daddy said. "Perhaps she feels shy in a place where people haven't known her all her life."

Mother shook her head. "Marguerite shy?" she said. "She never was before."

"Never was in a place where she had to put herself forward before," Daddy said.

"I hate California," Marguerite would say. "I hate school and I hate Stanley Avenue. I hate all the dull people and all the dull houses and all the dull days." And she would kick at a chair leg or slam doors until Mother spoke to her sharply and sent her outside.

But when the Hanisians moved into the neighborhood, Marguerite started acting more like her old self. She began to take an interest in things again. Mostly, she began to take an interest in Francie.

6

A Real Little Girl

"How do you do," Mrs. Hanisian said the first day we went to visit Francie. "Please come in." She stepped back from the door, gesturing gracefully with one slender, long-fingered hand.

Marguerite and I jostled against one another as we tripped over the doorstep in our nervousness. I tried not to stare about me, but I couldn't help notice that the inside of the Hanisian house was very different from ours, or any other house on the block for that matter. Oh, the rooms were the same size, and arranged in the same plan. The living room was to the right of the front door through an arch, the dining room to the left, and a narrow hall led to the bedrooms. But the furnishings and decorations were like none I had ever seen outside of the movies. The windows were swathed in great swatches of brocade and velvet and lace, and the light that filtered dimly through them illuminated furniture that was strangely carved and ornately inlaid. The walls were hung with paintings and tapestries in rich, dark colors—wine red and forest green and royal blue. All about, on little tables and odd little bric-a-brac shelves, stood porcelain figurines and marble statuettes and other unusual and interesting objects—a Japanese fan and a petit-point pincushion and a pair of brilliant blue butterflies suspended in a crystal globe. Walking into the Hanisian house was like entering Ali Baba's cave or a gypsy caravan. The place between my shoulders tingled with excitement. I looked at Marguerite and could see she was feeling the same sensation, though her eyes were fixed on the piano, gleaming magnificently in the shadowy living room.

"Francie hasn't ever had many playmates," Mrs. Hanisian was saying. "It is kind of you to come. Now, which of you is Marguerite? And which is Jeanne?" She had a strange, hesitant smile on her face, and her tone of voice was the same she might have used speaking to grown-ups.

I tore my eyes away from the wonders all about me and waited for Marguerite to answer. But Marguerite didn't seem to hear. She was still staring at the piano.

"Uh, this is Marguerite," I said, elbowing her hard. She whirled and glared at me, then remembered Mrs. Hanisian and forced herself to smile. "I'm Jeanne, but everyone calls me Jeannie," I said.

"How do you do," Marguerite murmured.

"I'm pleased to meet you both," Mrs. Hanisian said, and turned and led us down the hall.

Marie, the biggest girl, stood in the doorway of the

first bedroom. "Mamma," she said. "Mamma, you're not going to . . ."

Mrs. Hanisian's voice was firm and distant. "Not now, Marie," she said. She didn't look at Marie, but walked straight past her, then turned and beckoned to us once again. "This way, girls," she said.

I looked at Marie. Her face was sullen.

"Hi," I said, but she just looked at me for a moment, then turned and shut her door. Mrs. Hanisian did not seem to notice. She was walking through the open door at the end of the hall.

"Francie," I heard her say, "some neighbor girls have come to play with you—Marguerite and Jeannie Sloan from across the street."

Marguerite and I peered hesitantly into the room. Francie was in a wheelchair by the window. She bounced wildly against the straps that held her in and made strange, excited animal sounds. I noted with fascination that a thin thread of spittle drooled from one corner of her mouth. I stepped through the doorway, reaching out to pull Marguerite in with me.

"Hi," I said.

"She'll calm down in a moment," Mrs. Hanisian said. "Please don't be afraid. She's just glad to see you."

Marguerite and I nodded dumbly. I tried not to stare, but there seemed nowhere else to look except at the contorted little figure in the wheelchair. What are we going to *do* with her, I thought. I looked to Marguerite for help.

She was the oldest, after all.

Marguerite's lower lip was trembling, and her face was getting splotchy. Oh boy, I thought. Now what?

"Can we take Francie for a walk?" I blurted out, hardly knowing where the idea had come from before I had said it.

"I think that would be a fine thing to do," Mrs. Hanisian said. "I'll help you get the chair down the steps."

"We can pretend we're nurses," I told Marguerite as we wheeled the chair down the sidewalk. It was easier once we were out in the sunshine, away from the dim mystery of Francie's strange house. Walking behind Francie, where we didn't have to look at her, I felt much better. "She can be the patient," I said.

In the chair in front of us, Francie flailed and made noises. I was glad there were no other kids in sight on the street.

Marguerite was very quiet. She had not cried, as I had feared, but I could tell she was upset. "I think she's trying to say something," Marguerite whispered. Her face was wrinkled into a worried frown.

"Naw," I said, "she can't talk."

"Shhh!" Marguerite hissed. "She'll hear you."

"Marg, she can't understand what we say. You can tell. Just look at her!"

Marguerite looked at the back of Francie's head, lolling to one side. The straight dark hair stood on end. Francie bounced and grunted frantically.

"Listen," Marguerite whispered.

"Don't be silly."

"No, really," Marguerite said. "Listen."

I listened. Francie's noises increased in tempo and volume. "It's just a bunch of gibberish, Marg."

Marguerite stopped pushing. "I think she's trying to say something," she said stubbornly, and walked around to kneel before Francie's chair.

Francie's crooked little hands were waving in the air. She lunged toward Marguerite, mouthing unintelligible sounds. Only the leather straps that bound her to the chair kept her from crashing forward into Marguerite's lap. I watched, amazed, as Marguerite, lately so timid, reached out and grabbed Francie's chin, holding the bobbling head still, and looked questioningly into her eyes. Francie's voice stilled. Indeed, her whole frenetic body seemed to quiet. She grunted softly, and Marguerite looked up at me in wonder.

"She *is* talking," she said. "She's trying to tell us something. I know she is. Look!"

I came around the chair and knelt gingerly beside my sister. Francie's drooling mouth was twisted into a leering grin. Her hand jerked out and knocked roughly against my shoulder.

I heard Marguerite's voice, almost whispering. "Think what it must be," she said, and there was a little quiver in her voice, "think . . . to have no one, no one understand you."

Francie grunted and twisted her mouth painfully, mouthing a series of sounds that, no matter how hard I listened, sounded like gibberish to me.

"Never mind," Marguerite said to Francie, and she reached out and gave Francie's hand a squeeze. "Never mind. We'll try to figure out a way to understand." And then she said something that made no sense to me at all. "I know what it's like," she said to Francie, "when people don't understand. . . . We'll listen real hard, won't we, Jeannie?"

I looked from Marguerite, puzzled, into Francie's big blue eyes. For a moment, our eyes locked together in a long, unwavering stare. I felt my heart turn over, sick and heavy, in my chest. Deep within those eyes, looking out at me from that strangely old and distorted face, was a real girl.

"Yeah," I said. "Yeah, we'll listen. Sure we will."

7

Friends with Francie

WE SPENT a lot of time at the Hanisians' house that summer. Partly it was because we loved to look at all the strange and wonderful things they had and listen to Mrs. Hanisian play the piano and hear her talk of the glamorous life she had led. Partly it was because sometimes Marie or Zadora let us experiment with their nail polishes and face powders or read their movie magazines. But mostly it was because of the friendship that grew between Francie and Marguerite.

I think Marguerite liked the way Francie was always so glad to see her. From the day Marguerite took Francie's chin in her hand and first looked into her eyes, something special happened to Francie every time she saw Marguerite. It was as if a light switch was turned on somewhere inside of Francie. She just sort of began to glow: she followed Marguerite with her eyes and would get very still when Marguerite spoke, as if everything Marguerite said was important.

Unlike other kids we knew, Francie never had anything more interesting to do than to play with Marguerite and me. She was the most cooperative of playmates—willing to take any part in our games, no matter how unpopular, from "baby" when we played "house" to "bad guy" when we played "cops and robbers." She would let us dress her up in cast-off clothes or haul her along in my old baby carriage more docilely even than the Dooley baby would. And for Marguerite, who loved to read aloud, Francie was a never-tiring audience.

Marguerite began to come alive whenever she was with Francie. Her eyes began to sparkle, and she began to laugh again, her old magical laugh that made everyone who heard it feel good inside. I wished, sometimes, just a little, it had been *me* who made Marguerite laugh again.

Lots of times, I got tired of playing with Francie and wandered off in the company of the other kids. Marguerite always stayed. It was Marguerite who learned that Francie could nod her head "yes" and "no" in answer to our questions. Before long, Marguerite claimed she could understand some of what she insisted Francie was trying to say.

Francie was small and light, though she was older than me and almost as old as Marguerite. If I helped, Marguerite could lift Francie out of her chair, and they liked to lie together on a blanket under the lemon tree in Francie's back yard to "talk." I didn't have the patience for the slow word games Marguerite played with Francie, but Marguerite never seemed to tire of them.

"I worry about Marguerite," I heard Mother tell Daddy one day near the end of summer. "She spends all her time with the little Hanisian girl and never plays with the other children."

"She never played with them before," said Daddy. "If you ask me, one friend is better than none. Give her time. She acts happier than I've seen her since we moved from Oregon."

It was true. After Francie Hanisian moved into our neighborhood, Marguerite wasn't lonesome any more. She paid no attention to the other kids, and it was me who began to feel embarrassed about Francie.

"She makes Lloyd sick to his stomach," I had to tell her. "We've gotten used to Francie, Marguerite, and our mother likes her mother, but Mrs. Timothy thinks Francie should be in a home, and Mrs. Lord won't let Carol and Irene play with her."

"Honestly," said Marguerite. "You'd think she was catching! Well, I couldn't care less if they don't want to play with us—the stuck-up things!"

But I did care. I liked walking to the swimming pool, my suit rolled in a towel under my arm, with Louise and Alice Jane and Carol and Irene. I liked playing hide and seek after dinner in the dusky street. I liked borrowing Mrs. Dooley's baby and wheeling him downtown, sure passers-by thought he was my baby. And I liked the comfortable feeling of running and skipping, laughing and talking with children just like me.

When I looked into Francie's blue eyes, what I saw was hard to bear. I didn't like to think how it must feel to be Francie, trapped inside a body she couldn't control, unable to let people around her know what she felt and thought. And I understood why even Francie's sisters, Marie and Zadora, didn't like to take her with them when they walked downtown. I had come to know how uncomfortable it was to have people stare and whisper when they saw us wheel her down the street. There's nothing *I* can do about it, I would think angrily. I want to have some fun!

So often, when Marguerite and Francie were busy with their word games, I played with the other kids, and I even felt embarrassed when Sammy jeered, "Where's your sister? Playing with the idjit again!"

"Birds of a feather flock together," mocked Alice Jane, and the other kids laughed. I should have beaten them all up right then and there, and I felt like it too, only there were a bunch of them and just one of me, so I laughed too, and felt sick to my stomach.

"You stop that, you kids," I said, and I could feel the hot redness climb up my neck and into my face.

"Francie is going to miss you girls when you start back to school," Mrs. Hanisian said one day in late summer when she brought lemonade and cookies out to us in the yard. Marguerite and Francie and I had been "camping" in a tent made of blankets hung over the clothesline.

Marguerite munched thoughtfully on a cookie. "I don't suppose Francie can go to school," she said.

"No, I'm afraid not. They won't take her in public school, and a private one is out of the question."

Mrs. Hanisian was gathering up the glasses and napkins and putting them back on her tray, while I fed bites of cookie to Francie, so she wouldn't crumble them. Francie could feed herself, but she made an awful mess, so Marguerite and I often helped her just to avoid the cleaning up.

"Is that why Francie can't read and write?" Marguerite asked.

"Francie couldn't write in any case," Mrs. Hanisian said gently, pausing a moment by Francie's chair to look down at her and softly smooth her wild, dark hair. "She can't control her hands well enough. As for reading . . ."

"She loves stories," said Marguerite. "She likes me to hold the book where she can see. And she can control her hands to feed herself. I thought . . ."

"I really don't think so, dear," said Mrs. Hanisian. "It's hard to tell how much she understands. Because we're around her all the time, we've gotten to know what she means when she makes certain noises or gestures. Sometimes I think . . ." Her voice trailed off. Then she gave herself a little shake and picked up the tray. "No, the doctors have all said it's hopeless. It's sweet of you, dear, but . . . You'll just have to be sure to come over sometimes after school to read to her. She loves the attention. You girls have been kind to Francie, and I want you to know how much I appreciate it."

I loved it when Mrs. Hanisian talked to us like that. It made me feel grown up, for she never talked to us as if we were kids at all, but was just as polite, and interested in what we said as if we were adults. But this time, her words made me feel ashamed. I wished I had socked Alice Jane and Sammy on their noses.

"Francie understands lots," said Marguerite, looking fierce. "I just know she does."

Mrs. Hanisian's mouth smiled at us, but her eyes were sad.

"We *love* Francie," Marguerite said, and I nodded emphatically, vowing silently never again to let the kids tease me or Marguerite about Francie. "We'll come over real often," Marguerite said, "even after school starts, and read to Francie and play with her, just like always. Only . . ." Marguerite had a funny look in her eyes, and I had a feeling she wasn't going to let it go at that.

8

Teaching Francie

FRANCIE was sitting in her wheelchair on the porch of her house when we came out of our front door the first day of school. I waved to her and ran down the steps to join Louise and Alice Jane, who were waiting on the sidewalk. Francie looked small and forlorn, hunched in her chair, and her arm waved jerkily back at me. It made me feel kind of funny leaving her behind as we walked down the street to pick up the Lord girls. I saw Louise nudge Alice Jane and roll her eyes toward Francie, but they didn't say anything. I gave them a warning look and balled my fists at my side just in case, but they began to talk of something else.

Children were coming out of almost every house on the block. Marie and Zadora rattled by in a boyfriend's old roadster on their way to the high school. I could hear the Dooley baby bawling loudly from his playpen on their porch.

"He wants to go to school," explained Alice Jane. "He doesn't understand he's too little."

I wondered if Francie understood why she couldn't go to school. I didn't want to think about it, so I started talking fast to Alice Jane, making jokes about how someday the baby would be crying because he *had* to go to school. I didn't look back at Francie. I didn't want to see her sitting there, watching as we all walked away from her.

Marguerite wasn't talking or laughing at all. She walked ahead of us very fast, and her head was bowed. I could see that the back of her neck, visible where her blonde hair swung forward to hide her face, was splotched with red, and I knew, uncomfortably, that Marguerite was crying.

"Marguerite says you're to go home without her," Irene Lord told me after school that day.

"How come?"

"I dunno. She just said tell you. Come on, Jeannie. You can stop at our house on the way if you want. Mama's prob'ly got sugar bread or somethin', and I'm starved!" Irene's plump face was bright with anticipation, and my own stomach growled at the thought of Mrs. Lord's snacks. Mother only let us have an apple or some raisins after school. "So you won't spoil your supper," she would say. I fell into step with Irene and Carol.

"D'ya like Mrs. Nelson?" Carol asked. "I had her last year."

"She's OK," I said. "I just wish Marguerite hadn't been in her class. She gets such good grades; and then, when I come along behind her, pretty soon the teacher's saying to me, 'Are you *sure* you're Marguerite Sloan's sister?' "

"Speaking of Marguerite," said Louise Dooley, joining us and hauling her little brother along by the hand, "what's she doing down in the primary wing?"

"Search me!"

"I saw her go into Miss O'Brien's room just now when I went to get Eddie."

"Maybe she's gone back to first grade to brush up," wisecracked Carol, and we all laughed; but I wondered why Marguerite hadn't mentioned staying late. And what in the world was she doing in the first grade room?

"I WENT to get these," Marguerite said, in answer to my question later that afternoon. She dumped an armful of books on our bed. "Look. Miss O'Brien said I could borrow them, and when we're through with these, we can borrow more. She was really nice when I explained why we needed them." She plopped down beside the books and began sorting through them, holding them up one by one. "Look at this—an ABC book and a primary reader and . . . Look here, she even gave me some flash cards and some cut-out ABC's."

"Why *do* we need them?" I asked. "We already *know* how to read."

"But Francie doesn't," said Marguerite triumphantly, "and *we're* gonna teach her!"

To TELL the truth, it was Marguerite who did the teaching in the end. Oh, I tried, but it got to be so boring, going over to the Hanisians' every day after school. The other girls were always going skating or to the library or to the corner store, and I liked to go with them. But Marguerite would just say, "Francie's expecting me. You go on, Jeannie. They didn't invite *me* anyway." She didn't seem to understand they didn't invite her because she acted as if she didn't care about being with anyone but Francie.

Teaching Francie wasn't easy. It was hard for me to tell whether Francie even understood what Marguerite was telling her, but Marguerite insisted she did.

"Listen, Jeannie," she would say, and holding a book propped on Francie's wheelchair tray with one hand, she would point to a word. Sure enough, Francie's mouth would twist painfully around a garbled sound. Sometimes it *did* sound a little like the word Marguerite was pointing to. Marguerite said Francie was reading. Who was I to say she wasn't?

"What do you find to do with Francie every day?" Mother asked Marguerite.

"I *told* you, Mother. I'm teaching her to read."

The worried little frown creased Mother's forehead. "Oh, *that*," Mother said.

9

California Autumn

Sometimes on warm evenings, the sound of Mrs. Hanisian's piano would drift across the street and through our open windows. Marguerite and I loved to lie in bed and listen to the music, but often I was vaguely disturbed by it. Mrs. Hanisian's music throbbed with something I didn't understand. She would begin quietly, her technique perfect and controlled. In my mind's eye, I could see her beautiful long white fingers moving over the shining ivory keys. Mrs. Hanisian had short oval fingernails, buffed to a pearly glow. "A pianist's nails must not click on the keys," she had told Marguerite, and Marguerite had gone straight home to cut her nails and file them short and smooth. I did not need to cut mine, already bitten to the quick. But short nails or not, Marguerite and I had no piano to play, and so we listened to Mrs. Hanisian.

On those hot nights, imagining Mrs. Hanisian's hands touching the piano keys, I would hear how, little by little, the control in her playing would slip away. The music would grow wild, rising in a crescendo of intensity that would leave my heart pounding. There was an anguish, a restlessness, a sadness in Mrs. Hanisian's playing at night we never felt in the daytime Mrs. Hanisian, so regal and calm.

I can remember pressing my hands to my chest to feel how hard my heart was thumping when at last the piano would fall silent. The only sound on the still night air would be the singing of the cicadas in the lawn. Beside me, Marguerite lay motionless, and in the moonlight I could see that her cheeks were wet and her eyes stared sightlessly at the ceiling.

"Golly," I breathed, needing to break the quiet. I snuggled over close to Marguerite, and she reached for the handkerchief under her pillow and blew her nose.

"I wish . . ." Marguerite said in a choked whisper, "I wish I could play like that. Her music tells just how she feels—better than words, better than anything."

I lay very still, trying to understand. "It sounds . . . almost angry. . . ." I said.

I could feel Marguerite nod. "She probably misses playing before the crowned heads of Europe."

"Or she misses being rich," I said.

"Oh, Jeannie," Marguerite sighed. "Riches don't matter. But she had fame and love and beauty—"

"She's still beautiful, even if she is old."

"Yes, but she has no one to love her."

"Marie and Zadora love her . . . and Francie."

"Yes, but . . ." Marguerite sighed again deeply. "Oh,

Jeannie, you're just too *young* to understand."

IN A WAY, it was a relief when the evenings grew too chilly for open windows. Mrs. Hanisian's night music was beautiful, and we loved it. But it was more comfortable somehow not to hear it. When she played during the day, with the sun shining and the neighbors talking and moving about in their houses and lawn mowers and the automobiles over on Verdugo Boulevard making a background to the music, it was more like when Mrs. Sisson played—just another neighborhood sound, familiar and pleasant.

Marguerite and I had to wear sweaters now when we went outside to play, and some of the trees dropped their leaves, and on Saturdays you could smell them being burned on backyard bonfires.

Halloween came and went. Marguerite and I dressed up as gypsies in Mother's old skirts, with curtain rings tied to our ears and all Mother's beads bedecking our arms and necks. After the Halloween parade, Mrs. Lord gave us popcorn balls, and Mrs. Dooley gave apples, and Mrs. Hanisian had an etched brass tray from which she offered us foil-wrapped candies that were sticky and sugary and centered with a filling of chewy dates. Francie did not go to the parade or to ring doorbells with us, though Marguerite offered to take her. I was relieved when Mrs. Hanisian said no, Francie would stay home with her to give out treats.

IT WAS our second Thanksgiving in California. Mother roasted a duck someone had given to Daddy. It seemed strange to have Thanksgiving by ourselves. In Oregon there had always been lots of relatives for Thanksgiving, cousins and aunts and uncles and Grandmother Sloan. I could remember how the aunts laughed and talked together in the kitchen while they prepared the dinner. Marguerite and I used to crawl under the kitchen table, where we were out of the way, and listen. The uncles would sit in the living room, smoking pipes or cigars, and the air would be blue and smothery with the smoke, and the aunts would scold and open the front door, even though often it was raining or the wind was cold. In California, Mother fixed dinner with only Marguerite and me to help, and Daddy sat in the living room in a pool of warm sunshine by the window and read his paper and called out bits of the news to Mother as she worked.

Marguerite didn't like the duck. She said it was too greasy and made her stomach feel upset. But Daddy praised it and took third helpings of everything, and Mother's cheeks grew pink and she looked pleased. I finished up what was left on Marguerite's plate.

It seemed funny to have such a quiet dinner. When the dishes were done, Mother and Daddy took naps, and Marguerite and I cut out paper dolls. I hated paper dolls. My fingers went into cramps trying to cut all the tiny details, and Marguerite was so fussy about how they were done and wouldn't let me cut if I didn't do it just so. I wished I could go outdoors to play, but there was no one out there to play with. Mother said Thanksgiving was a family time, and everyone else was with their own families that day.

10

The Championship

"THE TROUBLE IS, Jeannie," Marguerite said to me one Saturday morning after Thanksgiving. "The trouble is no one but me and Mrs. Hanisian understands Francie when she talks, and no one but me knows she can read."

"I do," I said. "I know she can read."

"No, you don't. You just say that 'cause you think I want you to."

"Well . . ." I said, "I think maybe she can. It's so hard to tell. Now if she could talk . . . so's I could understand her, I mean . . . or write. . . ."

"If she could write, people would have to believe it. And it'd help her let us know when she wants something too. . . ." Marguerite's voice faded thoughtfully. She was lying on her stomach on our bed, her chin propped on her hands. I was sorting my jacks. I had lost parts of three different sets and was making up a new set out of what was left of the old ones.

"Mmmm," I said. "Do you have a jacks ball, Marg? Mine is somewhere, but I don't know where, and I play

Alice Jane for the block championship today."

Marguerite swung herself into a sitting position and slid off the bed to rummage in her closet. "Here," she said, handing me her ball. "Don't lose it too, OK? It's the only one I have."

"Mine's not lost. I just can't find it. Thanks," I said. "Are you coming to watch?"

Marguerite stood staring out of the window while I stuffed the ball and jacks into the little bag Mother had made for them.

"Marg? Are you?"

She looked at me questioningly, and I knew she had not even heard me.

"Are you coming to watch me beat Alice Jane?"

"Oh, no, Jeannie, I guess not. Francie's expecting me this morning for her lesson."

I jerked my sweater on over my head, feeling suddenly angry. "You know what Mrs. Hanisian said, Marg. Francie's hopeless. There's no way she can learn to write."

"There must be a way," Marguerite said, not noticing my anger. She had turned once again to the closet and was groping for her own sweater. "There's just gotta be a way," she said.

I don't know why I said it, except I felt right then my own sister was letting me down. She seemed to care more about Francie than she did about me. After all, she ought to know what the championship meant to me. I wasn't good at a lot of things, but I *was* good at jacks. The contest had been my idea, and almost every girl in the neighborhood had joined in; but now only Alice Jane and I were unbeaten. We had agreed to meet that day for a final championship match. All the kids would be there to watch. All but Marguerite. I don't know why, but before I even knew what I was going to say, the awful words were out of my mouth.

"Give up, Marg," I said, stomping to the door. "Give up, why don't you. You're never going to teach that dummy anything!"

As soon as I heard myself saying it, I wished I could call the words back. They hung in the air between us, ugly and cruel. I could not bear to turn around and see the shock I knew would be in Marguerite's eyes. I slammed the door and ran down the hall, my words echoing sickeningly in my ears.

ALL THE KIDS *were* there. Especially the Dooleys. Even the baby, Gerald, was there, astride Louise's hip. When she set him down, he crawled straight for the street, so she ended up holding him. He wiggled and squirmed and pulled her hair and fussed, but Louise struggled with him alone. Alice Jane was practicing, and Alexander wouldn't help. He just slouched around the edges of the group of kids, pretending he wasn't watching, the way boys do.

At least he came, I thought. I tried to feel justified in what I had said to Marguerite. Before Francie moved to the neighborhood, *I* was Marguerite's best friend, I thought. It's all Francie's fault. But somehow I couldn't feel mad at Francie, and the sick feeling in the pit of my stomach wouldn't go away.

"OK, kids," yelled Carol Lord, who had appointed herself referee when she was the first to lose. Carol and Irene were too plump to be good at games. Even in sitting-down games, like jacks, they were hindered by their short, stubby fingers. "OK, kids," Carol yelled. "Take your places."

Alice Jane plunked herself down across from where I stood and pulled her dress down so her panties wouldn't show. She rubbed her hands on her knees and emptied her jacks bag on the pavement. A golf ball fell out.

"No fair," I said. "I thought we agreed, golf balls bounce too high."

"That's a stupid rule," said Alice Jane, narrowing her eyes at me. "A golf ball makes the game more interesting."

The kids were quiet, waiting to see what was going to happen. I stared back at Alice Jane.

"Both play with golf balls, or nobody," said Carol. I thought Carol probably hoped I'd win.

"I don't have a golf ball," I said.

Alice Jane smiled sweetly and reached into her pocket. "I just happen to have two," she said.

I reluctantly took the ball she held out to me and noticed for the first time how long and skinny her fingers were.

I weighed the ball in my hand and crouched down on the pavement, trying to arrange my legs under me comfortably. My knee smarted from where I had last skinned it. The sick feeling in my stomach got worse. I wished Marguerite was there.

Alice Jane sat easily, her legs spread wide. She picked up her jacks and held them on her spread-open palms and tossed them into the air. She caught all but one on the backs of her hands. She tossed them again, this time from the backs, and caught all of the remaining jacks on her palms.

I repeated the ritual, but on the second toss only four jacks remained in my hands.

"Me first," said Alice Jane, and grinned.

Thunk. Grab. Catch. Thunk. Grab. Catch. Alice Jane played rhythmically, right through the Baby Game and Downs and Ups. I watched, my heart sinking as she began Eggs in the Basket. She scattered her jacks, tossed her ball, grabbed a jack, and as the ball came down, thunk, she transferred the jack to her other hand and caught the ball before it could bounce again. Toss. Grab. Thunk, transfer, and catch. Toss. Grab. Thunk, transfer, and catch. She didn't miss until sixsies.

I swallowed hard and began the Baby Game.

The kids stood and knelt in a circle around us. Whenever Alice Jane had finished a bounce, the Dooleys had cheered, even Gerald. Irene and little Delores Benjamin were rooting for me, but the boys, except for the Dooley boys, acted like they didn't care who won.

"Yay!" Irene would yell when my hand came up triumphantly filled with jacks and ball, but Delores forgot sometimes and cheered at the wrong places, so my supporters sounded a little weak. I was flushed and breathing hard by the time I missed twosies in Crack the Eggs. I rocked back and stretched my legs, smiling a little, and waited to see what Alice Jane could do.

Alice Jane played straight through Crack the Eggs, Upcast, and Downcast without missing a beat. It was foursies on Pigs in the Pen that got her.

I took a deep breath and leaned forward to play. I nearly lost my balance, lunging for a wild bounce on the Downcast game. The high bounce of the golf ball was hard to get used to, but I congratulated myself I was doing pretty well. I could feel the sweat on my upper lip and under my arms as I cupped my left hand on the pavement and began Pigs in the Pen. It was foursies that tripped me up too.

Alice Jane had begun to breathe hard. I could see she hadn't reckoned on my being so good. Thunk. Swoosh. Grab. Thunk. Swoosh. Grab. She finished out Pigs in the Pen and began Sweeps. I was ready to cry by the time she got to Bounce, No Bounce. I hadn't dreamed she could go clear from Pigs in the Pen to the very last game without missing, all in one turn. When she missed on fivesies, I almost did cry . . . from relief.

Thunk. Swoosh. Grab. Five pigs in the pen.

Thunk. Swoosh. Grab. I held up six jacks.

If she can do it, I can do it, I told myself, and I didn't even pause for breath as I began Sweeps.

My heart was pounding so loudly I thought all the kids could hear it. I had played straight through to Bounce, No Bounce too.

Toss. Grab. Thunk. Catch. Toss, transfer and catch.

"Onesies!" shouted Irene, and Delores yelled, "Yay!"

Toss. Grab. Thunk. Catch. Toss, transfer, and catch.

"Twosies!"

"Yay!"

Toss. Grab. Thunk. Catch. Toss, transfer, and . . . Thunk. I stared helplessly at the ball, which continued to bounce in lower and lower arcs. My hand was empty.

Alice Jane leaned forward, a look of concentration on her freckled face. The kids were absolutely still. It was as if they were holding their breath.

Toss. Grab. Thunk. Catch. Toss, transfer and catch.

"Fivesies!" the Dooleys yelled.

Alice Jane stretched her shoulders and arched her back. She leaned forward, breathing through her mouth, and the tip of her tongue stuck out pink from a gap in her teeth.

Toss. Grab. Thunk. Catch. Toss, transfer, and catch. Alice Jane's left hand came up and opened. Six jacks winked at me from her palm. The ball was secure in her other hand.

"Good game," said Alice Jane in a condescending voice, dropping the ball and holding out her hand.

The Dooleys cheered.

11

Real Words

I LET MYSELF into the house by the back door. I had seen Daddy out working in the front yard pansy bed, pulling up faded plants, so I cut through Mendenhall's back lot. I didn't want him to see me coming home. I wasn't ready to talk to anyone about the game, not even Daddy. It had been all I could do to pretend to congratulate Alice Jane on her victory. I had been so sure I would win!

I could hear someone in the kitchen—Marguerite, I guessed, because I could see Mother napping on the daybed in the den, with an afghan thrown across her legs. I tiptoed past the kitchen door. I especially didn't want to see Marguerite. Wish she was still at Francie's, I thought. That's where she likes to be anyway. I was trying just as hard as I could to be mad at Marguerite, but the truth was, more than my scraped and stinging hand was sore. More even than my pride. My conscience hurt.

I opened the door to the room Marguerite and I shared and looked straight into the wide blue eyes of Francie, whose wheelchair was parked squarely inside our door. Her face lit up the way it always did when she saw me or Marguerite, and she began to bounce in her chair, making the little mewing sounds I knew by now meant pleasure.

"Francie!" I said. "What are you doing here?" and without knowing why, I burst into tears.

Francie's glad face changed immediately. The wide, drooling smile turned down at the corners, and her blue eyes filled with tears. Flailing, she reached her skinny little arms out to me. I stumbled to her chair and dropped to my knees in front of her, burying my head in her lap. I couldn't help myself. I cried and cried, I don't know how long, and all the while, Francie's spastic little hands thumped gently against my back.

At last I pulled myself together and lifted my head. Francie searched my face, her own face twisted in distress.

"Whaz-ma-dah!" I heard her cry, over and over. "Whaz-ma-dah, Jee-nee? Whaz-ma-dah?"

And I understood! For the first time I heard what Marguerite had heard. The thick and halting sounds that Francie made were words, real words!

"Nothing," I said. "Nothing's the matter now, Francie. Nothing at all."

"GOLLY, I'm sorry, Jeannie," said Marguerite. "I guess I wasn't thinking what it meant to you—the jacks game, I mean. I was so busy trying to think how to help Francie."

She had found Francie and me, laughing and crying

and hugging all at once, when she came back to our room with the tray of cookies and hot chocolate she had been fixing in the kitchen.

"It doesn't matter," I said, shaking my head, and I meant it too. "It really doesn't matter. I'm just so sorry what I said. I deserved to lose. What matters is I know Francie can talk. I can hear her. She really can talk."

Marguerite looked glad, and Francie was grinning at us both, joggling her head. "Dode-fee-bahd, Jee-nee," Francie said. "Dad-Allus-Jade-hahds-too-big!"

"Huh?" I said.

"Hahds-too-big!"

Marguerite laughed. "She says Alice Jane's hands are too big and she's right. No matter how well you played, Jeannie, your hands aren't as big as Alice Jane's. She's got such skinny, long fingers, I bet she could go to twelvsies if she tried. Your hands won't hold that many jacks. It's not that she's better—just bigger. So there's no reason to feel bad."

And I didn't feel bad any more, but it didn't have a thing to do with Alice Jane Dooley *or* her snaky fingers. The sick feeling in my stomach was gone. In fact, I felt so hungry I ate most of the cookies.

Francie and Marguerite and I couldn't seem to do anything but laugh. I told them how Delores kept yelling "Yay!" before I would even have a chance to bounce my ball, and how I'd almost fallen over once, and how, when Louise got excited and put Gerald down to hug Alice Jane when she won, Gerald crawled right into the middle of things and tried to eat a jack. Everything was funny. And when I held up Francie's hot chocolate cup so she could drink, and I took it away, and a glob of marshmallow, all sticky and gooey, was stuck to her nose, I thought we'd all die of the laughing.

"I WISH everyone understood when Francie talks," I said that night, snuggled warm and cozy beside Marguerite in bed.

"She's getting better every day," said Marguerite. "She practices and practices."

"Yeah . . ." I said, thinking hard about what had made me hear Francie's words. "Yeah . . ." I said, "but they've got to listen, too."

12

Marguerite's Idea

"I ALMOST DREAD Christmas this year," Mother said one night at dinner. "Holidays seem so lonely here—away from the family." Her voice was wistful, and she sighed as she stirred a spoonful of sugar into her tea.

I knew what she meant, and so, I guessed, did Marguerite, who was staring at her green beans with unfocused eyes. But Daddy glanced up, startled by Mother's words.

"Dread Christmas?" His voice sounded puzzled. It seemed to take him a moment to realize what Mother had said. "Why, Edith," he said. "How can you dread Christmas? We always have a fine time."

"Yes . . ." said Mother. "But down here holidays are so quiet. No one to share with. Christmas is a family time, and down here we have no family. . . ."

"We have each other," Daddy reproached her.

"Of course we do. It's just that I miss Faith and Len . . . and Chessie and Helga and the children . . . and Mother Sloan and your folks . . . Samuel and Eleanor and Barbara Faith. . . . Oh, everybody. The way it used

to be. Folks dropping in, and a big party on Christmas
Eve and, oh, I don't know . . . the uproar, I guess." She
laughed ruefully.

I felt a lump coming up in my throat at the picture
her words conjured in my head—a picture of Christmas in
Oregon, a houseful of people, people we belonged to and
who belonged to us. I even found myself thinking of our
prissy little cousin, Barbara Faith. She *was* pretty, with
her round blue eyes and her bouncing yellow curls, and
by now she might even be fun to play with. . . .

I looked across the table at Marguerite. Her head
was bowed over her plate.

Daddy looked at Mother. She waved her hand like
she was shooing a fly and put her napkin to her lips. He
looked at Marguerite. He looked at me.

"I didn't think," he said. "Of course it's lonesome,
spending Christmas by ourselves." He tapped his fork
handle thoughtfully on the table. "Well then, let's go to
Oregon for Christmas this year!"

I grinned at Daddy hopefully. Marguerite's head
flew up.

"Oh, Daddy, could we!" she breathed.

"Of course we couldn't," Mother said crossly. "Don't
talk nonsense, Ben. Train fare is scandalously expensive.
You know we can't afford. . . . I'm sorry I said a thing.
I was just thinking out loud, for heaven's sake. Don't go
getting the children's hopes up over nothing." She jumped
up and began clanking plates together angrily. "I declare,

you're a child yourself sometimes!" she said. "Come, girls, help clear the table."

"Now, Edith," Daddy protested gently, "I only thought . . ."

Mother stopped halfway to the kitchen and turned, her hands piled with the dishes she had gathered up. "You didn't think, Ben. That's the trouble. You didn't think at all!"

Marguerite and I pushed back our chairs, trying not to let them scrape against the floor. We began to clear the table, tiptoeing and hoping Mother and Daddy wouldn't notice us. We needn't have worried about Daddy. He sat in his place at the head of the table, drawing designs on the tablecloth with his fork handle. His face was heavy and sad, and he shook his head slowly back and forth, his lips pressed together tightly. I stopped by his chair for a moment, and before I reached for his tumbler, I put my hand on his sleeve. He reached over to pat it absent-mindedly, but he didn't look at me and he didn't stop drawing the fork over the tablecloth, slowly and thoughtfully.

MARGUERITE lifted the covers on her side of the bed and crawled in under them. I turned on my side to watch her. She settled her head on the pillow and smoothed the top of the sheet down over the blanket and pulled them both neatly up under her chin. Her eyes were sad and thoughtful as she reached above our heads to pull the chain on the reading lamp. With a rattle, the room went dark.

I waited for my eyes to adjust to the darkness. Little by little, the pale square of the window became visible, and I could see the shadows of the dressing table and the chest of drawers and the bookshelves against the walls. On Marguerite's side of the room the floor was clear and clean. The dolls and games and books were neatly lined up on her shelves. Her clothes were folded and put away. My side was a jumble—undressed dolls, some of them upside down, scattered and open books, and tiddlywinks strewn on the floor. My dress was in a heap in the corner and my sweater hung from the bedpost.

I wished Marguerite had nagged me to straighten up before we went to bed, the way she usually did. I wished she would whisper to me now in the dark. She had been quiet all evening, but then, so had I. We had done our homework in silence, and afterwards Marguerite had gotten out her paint set and painted a gloomy picture, all blues and greens and grays, that I glimpsed over her shoulder, though she wouldn't show it to me and ripped it up as soon as it was done. I had tried to play tiddlywinks by myself, but I kept getting confused, and in the end I had given it up and put on my nightgown early and climbed into bed. Mother had gone to her room with a headache right after the dishes were done, and Daddy had gone out to see someone about business. He had not come back, and I kept listening for him. I wished I would hear the front door open and Mother's voice calling, "That you, sweetheart?" But the house was silent, and the window, closed against the evening chill, muffled even the traffic sounds from Verdugo Boulevard.

"You asleep?" I whispered to Marguerite.

"No."

"Me neither."

Again there was silence.

"Marg?"

"What?" She sounded cranky.

"Nothing."

"Go to sleep."

"I can't."

"I know. I can't either."

"Marg, spoon with me." I needed to feel close to someone. I needed to block away the sad, lonely feeling that had been with me all evening.

Marguerite turned toward me. I snuggled against her, feeling her warmth all along my legs and back. She put her arm over me and nuzzled her face into my hair, and we lay together, my body curled into the curve of hers, like two spoons nestled in a silver chest.

"Know what I wish? said Marguerite softly.

"What?"

"I wish Francie was our cousin and Mrs. Hanisian was our aunt. Then *they* could have Christmas with us, and we wouldn't be alone and neither would they."

"Marie and Zadora, too?"

"Sure, them too. It would make it feel more like Christmas. I love Francie more than I love some of our dumb cousins anyway—more than I love Barbara Faith."

"I wouldn't mind having Mrs. Hanisian for an aunt," I said. "She's nice!" I tried the sound of it. "Aunt Mrs. Hanisian . . ." I said dreamily.

Marguerite giggled. "Silly! It would be Aunt Frances."

"Is that her name?"

"Um-hmm. Francie is named for her. Zadora told me."

"Aunt Frances . . ." I said. "That sounds nice."

I thought about it, about how Mrs. Hanisian—Aunt Frances—would talk to Mother while they stuffed the turkey and about playing with Francie or listening to Marie and Zadora talk, but anyway having them with us, all together on Christmas Eve. I drifted lazily into a dream of it, cuddled warm in Marguerite's arms. The house would be full of voices—laughing, caroling, chattering voices—and the good smells of turkey and fresh-baked cookies and pumpkin pie, and the sparkle of candlelight on silver and crystal and the lights on the tree. . . .

13

Everybody for Christmas

THE CLICK of the latch on the front door brought me instantly awake. I held my breath, heart thumping, and listened for Mother's call. I heard only the whispery sounds Daddy's coat made as he hung it on the coat-tree, and the heavy tread of his shoes on the floor as he felt his way down the darkened hallway. I could feel Marguerite's body, tense and listening, too. Daddy's footsteps stopped outside our door. We heard the knob turn and saw the door swing slowly inward. Daddy peeked in around the door.

I was so glad to see the burly dark shadow of his head and shoulders leaning around our door, I was out of bed in a minute, flinging the covers back over Marguerite, and half-fell, half-ran into Daddy's open arms.

"Daddy, Daddy, Daddy," I whispered.

"Hey!" Marguerite was flailing out from under the blankets I had thrown over her head. "Hey!" And then she too was in his arms, and he was sitting on the edge of our bed, one of us on each knee.

"You're getting too big for this, girls." He laughed.

"I think you're breaking my legs. I may be a cripple for life."

" 'Cripple' reminds me," I said, ignoring Marguerite's pained yelp. "Marguerite had a good idea. Could we invite the Hanisians for Christmas Eve? Then it wouldn't be so lonesome . . . for us *or* for them."

Marguerite and I watched his face as he considered the thought. A good thing about Daddy was he never just said no without thinking the way most grown-ups did. He always listened and thought before he answered.

"Marguerite," said Daddy, looking her seriously in the eye. "That is not a good idea."

Marguerite flushed and bit her lip, and I opened my mouth to protest.

"That is a *great* idea!" Daddy shouted. "That's the best idea I've heard." He hugged Marguerite and me in a great big tangled-up hug that took my breath away. "That is a *wonderful* idea," Daddy said, "and it gives me an even better one: Why not invite *everybody* for Christmas Eve? Everybody on the block—the Timothys and the Mendenhalls . . ."

"And the Hanisians," said Marguerite.

"Of course the Hanisians. And the Dooleys . . ."

"All of them?" I asked.

"Every single one, even the little fellow, what's his name?"

"Gerald."

"Even Gerald. And the Lords and the Sissons—"

"Do we have to invite Sammy Benjamin?" said Marguerite doubtfully.

"Yes, Sammy Benjamin and his little sister and Mr. and Mrs. Benjamin and . . . who else?"

"Did you say the Lords?"

"Yes, the Lords."

"Then that's all, all that live on the block," said Marguerite.

"How will we get them all in the house?" I said.

"The more the merrier!" said Daddy. "Why, I'll bet we're all in the same boat. Almost everyone in this neighborhood comes from some other place. Probably no one has kin nearby. Why *not* get together for a great big, old-fashioned family Christmas? Why not?" Daddy was chuckling and hugging us over and over again. "It'll be the best Christmas ever!"

"What will be the best Christmas ever?" said Mother sternly, from the doorway.

Daddy looked up, abashed.

"Did we wake you, Edith? I'm sorry."

Mother came into the room. She was wearing her pretty rose satin kimono, the one Daddy gave her for her birthday. Her face looked very pale and sad, and her eyes were dark-lidded and glistening.

"I wasn't asleep," she said, and sat down in our little rocking chair. "What will be the best Christmas ever?"

"Well," said Daddy, "the girls and I had an idea."

"It was just an idea," mumbled Marguerite.

"As a matter of fact, Marguerite had the first idea," said Daddy, "and it gave me an even bigger one."

"It would," said Mother wryly.

I couldn't wait. It was taking him so long to tell it. "We're going to invite the whole neighborhood for Christmas Eve," I said. "Francie and Mrs. Hanisian and all the Dooleys, even Gerald, and Sammy and his folks, and Carol and Irene and Mrs. Sisson and, and, and . . . just everybody!"

"Of course, it would have to be all right with you," Daddy said gently. "What do you think, Edith? I reckon almost everyone in the neighborhood is far from family, just like us. Maybe they all feel the way we do, sad and lonesome at holiday time. If we all got together, it would be a little like a big family party. What do you say?"

"Well . . ." said Mother.

"A whole houseful of people," I said. "Just like aunts and uncles and cousins, only neighbors instead."

"It would have to be potluck," said Mother, frowning. "I couldn't fix for that big crowd all by myself."

"Of course potluck," said Daddy. "Everyone would bring something, and the girls and I will help clean and decorate the house."

"The house is awfully small. . . ."

"The weather is mild here. The children could play out of doors. You wanted an uproar," said Daddy.

"I don't even *know* some of our neighbors very well," said Mother. "They're all so different from the folks back home. They might not feel at ease. . . ."

"There's no better time than Christmas to get to know each other," said Daddy firmly.

Mother looked at him, and I saw her face, which she had been holding stiff and cold against him, soften. The little frown between her brows smoothed, and her lips curved gently, trembling.

"Oh, Ben," she said. "Oh, all right. I suppose it might be fun."

She smiled, and Daddy grinned at her. I felt something that had been clutching in my chest ever since dinnertime loosen as he swung me over to sit beside Marguerite in the curve of one arm. He held out the other arm to Mother, and she got up from the rocking chair and came to us, a little shyly, I thought, and put her arms around his neck. Then Daddy pulled her into our hug, and squeezed together, we began to laugh.

14

Just Like Us

AND THAT'S HOW it happened that our second Christmas in California included every family on Stanley Avenue. Mother said she was surprised at the way everyone seemed to like the idea. "Why, they just jump at the chance to join in," she said, shaking her head. "You certainly were right, Ben. Everyone has been lonely at holiday times, just like us."

"Just like us," I said to Marguerite. "You always said everyone on Stanley Avenue was just like us."

Marguerite looked at me strangely. "Yes . . ." she said, sounding uncertain. "Yes, just like us, except . . ." I knew she was thinking of all the things we had learned about our neighbors since we invited them to the Christmas party.

"Vat a nice idea!" Mrs. Mendenhall had exclaimed, her round face beaming. "Like in de old country . . . ven de whole village enchoyed togedder. Christmas vas such a happy time den. . . ." Mrs. Mendenhall's voice trailed off, her eyes fixed on some distant time and place we could not see. "Und Varren vill enchoy it so, von't he, Papa?"

We looked at Mr. Mendenhall, who nodded, smiling, his pipe clamped between his teeth.

"Ya, ya," he said. "Varren iss too much alone."

"I didn't know the Mendenhalls came from Germany," I said to Marguerite. "Did you?"

"No," said Marguerite. "I guess I didn't think about it."

The Timothys didn't come from England, but Mr. Timothy's parents had. That was why Mr. Timothy said he would make real English wassail for the party and a flaming plum pudding.

"Just like Dickens," said Marguerite.

Mother was embarrassed about the Benjamins. "I should have realized," she said. "It just didn't occur to me."

But the Benjamins wanted to come to the party too.

"So?" said Mrs. Benjamin. "Jews have a holiday too this time of year—Chanukah. I'll bring a traditional Chanukah dish, latkes—what you call potato pancakes."

"Until you've tasted Eva's latkes with sour cream," said Mr. Benjamin, "you haven't lived."

"We'll find out about Christmas," said Mrs. Benjamin. "You'll find out about Chanukah. We'll celebrate together. Neighbors should know one another already."

But it was Mrs. Hanisian who surprised us most of all.

"I knew Marie and Zadora were embarrassed sometimes about Francie," Marguerite said, "but Mrs. Hanisian?"

"Who'd have guessed?" I agreed.

"Marie and Zadora would love to come, I know," Mrs. Hanisian had said, "but sometimes people . . . I mean, Francie . . . I mean. . . . Perhaps Francie and I had better not. . . . Thank you so much."

"But Francie's the reason for this party in the first place," said Daddy. "The girls wanted Francie first of all. The rest of the neighbors were an afterthought."

I looked at Mrs. Hanisian and was dismayed to see tears spilling from her beautiful blue eyes, eyes like Francie's. "It's different when Francie cries, when a *kid* cries," I tried to explain to Marguerite later. "When grown-ups cry, it feels scary. . . . It doesn't feel right somehow. . . . *Especially* Mrs. Hanisian."

Marguerite nodded slowly. "It makes her seem . . . real," she said softly, and that made me think. Did we think she wasn't real? I wondered. A movie star or a character in a book?

"I guess she's just . . . a person," I said to Marguerite. "Just like anybody . . . just, yes, real."

When Mrs. Hanisian began to cry, Daddy fumbled for his handkerchief and offered it to her, and Mother went to sit beside her on the sofa and put her arms around her. "Perhaps you girls should go tell Francie and Marie and Zadora about the party," Mother said to us over Mrs.

Hanisian's head, and we knew it was more a command than a suggestion. But we also knew Francie would come to the party if Mother had her way, and Mother usually did.

THE QUESTION of Francie and a present might have been a problem. Daddy had printed the name of every grown-up and child who was coming to the party on little slips of paper and had shaken them up in his hat. "We'll draw names for presents," he said. "There have to be presents at a Christmas party."

"But what about Francie?" Mother wanted to know. "We can scarcely expect the child to make or buy a present for someone."

Daddy frowned. "Not having a present to give might make her feel bad," he said.

"Francie could give a present to her mother," said Marguerite, and we looked at her in surprise.

"What?" I asked.

"It's a surprise," Marguerite said. "A surprise for Mrs. Hanisian."

"We could take Mrs. Hanisian's name out of the hat first, I suppose, and give it to Francie," said Mother. "It's not quite fair, but—"

"But this is a special circumstance," said Daddy. "We'll let Francie's present be for her mother."

"But what *is* it?" I wanted to know, when Marguerite and I were alone. "You can tell *me*."

Marguerite shook her head stubbornly, swinging her wavy, honey-colored hair. "I can't tell," she said. "I promised." And that was all I could get out of her, no matter how hard I begged.

I drew Alice Jane Dooley's name out of the hat. It was easy to think of a present for *her*. I just shook some pennies I had been saving out of the pottery pig Mother had bought for me on Olvera Street and bought her a new set of jacks at the five and dime. Mother helped me sew a little bag for her to keep them in from the scraps of my red plaid dress. Lumpy with the jacks and the little *rubber* ball and drawn tight at the top with a piece of gold cord, it looked real nice, just the right sort of gift for the jacks champion of Stanley Avenue.

Marguerite drew Sammy Benjamin's name.

"Do I have to?" she wailed to Daddy.

"You have to," said Daddy firmly.

"But I don't know what boys like," said Marguerite.

"Sheet music," said Mother. "Sammy plays the piano beautifully. He can always use new sheet music."

Marguerite was sullen, and I knew what she was thinking. "It's not fair," she said later. "He gets to play the piano and I don't, and then *I* have to give *him* sheet music. It's not fair!"

But the funny thing was, once Marguerite was in the music store, she took a long time picking out the piece to buy for him, and I noticed she chose the prettiest paper we had to wrap it in—the paper printed with bright red holly berries and spiky green holly leaves. And she found a real sprig of holly to tie on the package. "Why, Marguerite," said Mother, "what an artistic-looking package! You really have quite a flair!"

"LET'S PAINT a Merry Christmas sign to hang over the door," I suggested to Marguerite, when we were gluing paper chains and cutting out tinfoil stars for decorations.

"I don't have my paints any more," said Marguerite. "We'll have to draw it with crayon."

"But paint would be brighter. Your set was almost new. Where is it anyway?"

"I just don't have it right now," Marguerite said, and she wouldn't say anything more.

WE WERE all busy getting ready for the party, but Marguerite seemed busiest of all because she still went after school every day to Francie's house. The last week before Christmas, she started going over after dinner, too.

"I'm helping Francie with her present," I heard Marguerite tell Mother. "Please, Mother, let me go. She's working so hard, but she needs my help. Everything's so hard for Francie, it takes a long time."

Mother sighed. "Are you sure it was a good idea to encourage Francie to give a present, Marguerite?" she said.

"She can do it, Mother. Honest she can. She's working so hard."

"Oh, Marguerite," Mother said, "I know you like Francie, dear, but everyone has limitations, and Francie is far more limited than anyone you've ever known. You can't expect her to be like other children."

"I don't, Mother. Truly I don't. I just want to help her do what she wants to do." Marguerite's voice was trembling. "I just want to help."

15

The Party

THE PARTY turned out to be even better than I had imagined. "It feels like Christmas, really and truly," Marguerite said, cocking her head to one side to listen to the happy sounds. I breathed in deeply the fragrant smells that filled the house.

From the kitchen we could hear a murmur, pleasant and motherly, and smell a steamy spiciness that wafted through the swinging kitchen door. From outside, the hilarious shouts and scuffle of the neighborhood boys, playing Red Rover in the window-lit yard, drifted in to us. And from the living room, an agreeable grumble rose above the blue haze of smoke that drifted round the fathers' heads.

In our room, the neighborhood girls were gathered. They curled, giggling, on the bed and chairs, and the shrill sound of their voices escalated as dinnertime neared.

I looked around me in satisfaction, feeling proud and important, a "hostess," as Mother had assured us, of this very special occasion. All the girls were dressed in their best. Louise and Alice Jane Dooley and their little sister, Joycie, were astonishing in identical heaps of pink taffeta ruffles from which their knobby, freckled arms and legs emerged at odd, awkward angles.

"For goodness sakes!" whispered Marguerite, wide-eyed, when we first saw them coming up the walk.

"Pa got the material from the costume department," Louise said, primping, "and Ma copied one of Mary Pickford's dresses."

"Amazing!" said Marguerite.

Little Delores Benjamin was adorable in brown velvet and black patent leather Mary Janes tied with brown bows, and the Lord girls were chubbily romantic in ample white voile and pastel satin sashes.

I couldn't help admiring myself in the mirror over the dressing table. I was as pretty as Marguerite for once, I decided. Her dress was just like mine, only blue, made especially for the Christmas party. "Red is for brunettes, blue for blondes," Mother said, and so this time I was glad my hair was shiny brown instead of wavy gold like Marguerite's. My lace collar and little sparkly buttons showed bright against my red velveteen. Red is for Christmas, I thought. Marguerite might look like an angel as usual, but that was OK, because I was "like a holly berry," said Daddy. "My own, happy, rosy red holly berry." For Christmas, it seemed to me, that was just the way I wanted to look.

Marguerite had not joined in the chatter of the other

girls. She had excused herself to go help Mother, only Mother had sent her back to our room. "A hostess must entertain her guests," Mother said.

"Francie's *my* guest," said Marguerite under her breath; and so she went to sit quietly in a corner, looking as if she wished she weren't there, and the girls ignored her. Every once in a while, she would run to peer out of the narrow French window beside the front door. Everyone had arrived except the Hanisians.

"I wonder if she changed her mind," Marguerite fretted, when I tried to get her to join a game of Parcheesi some of the older girls were starting. "Maybe Mrs. Hanisian decided not to come after all."

"Not a chance," I assured her, but I wasn't so sure. I was halfway beginning to wish the Hanisians wouldn't come, much as I liked them. Everyone seemed to *belong* at our party, even the Benjamins. "For us, that must be a Chanukah bush," Mr. Benjamin had joked, admiring our Christmas tree, and everyone had laughed. I wondered if the Hanisians would fit in as well, if the other mothers would be comfortable in the face of Mrs. Hanisian's aloof glamour, if the other girls would giggle and talk so easily if Francie were in the room. "Not a chance," I told Marguerite, and halfway hoped there *was* a chance Mrs. Hanisian had changed her mind.

Watching for them the way we were, I don't know how they got into the house without our knowing, but suddenly I realized the voices of the girls were trailing off in confusion. "So I just told her . . ." I heard Carol Lord say, and then, in the midst of an empty silence, I looked up to see Marie and Zadora standing in the doorway behind Francie's high-backed wheelchair.

Marie and Zadora looked beautiful and grown-up in slender dresses of vivid georgette. Marie's hair was swirled into a deep wave over one eye, like a sleek and shining cap, and Zadora's ears sparkled with tiny ruby earrings, which matched her ruby dress. But Francie looked strange indeed.

"Mamma tried to dress her up," Zadora confided later, "but it's so hard. . . ."

"Francie *feels* dressed up," said Marguerite. "That's what counts."

The thin blue dress Francie wore only emphasized her humpy, twisted little back and her skinny little arms and legs. Her wild, dark hair had been slicked back from her forehead and tied with an enormous blue bow, so that her head seemed more topheavy than ever on her spindly neck. Without the usual fringe of spiky hair, her face looked even older and more distorted. And to make it worse, she was grinning her lopsided grin and jumping and lunging in her chair against the heavy leather straps that held her safe. In the quiet that had fallen on the room, her voice sounded weird and garbled, like some strange caged bird, crying to be free.

My eyes darted around the room, hoping against hope to find a face that was not shocked or embarrassed. "I didn't know *she* was invited," I heard someone whisper behind me, and I felt my ears burn.

"Hi," I said, and my voice sounded trembly and weak.

Marie and Zadora didn't answer. They stared, stony-faced, over our heads, and Marie tapped one foot nervously on the floor.

"Hey!" yelled Francie, grinning, and I was caught by the joy in her eyes.

Marguerite got up from the chair in the corner. She was careful not to look at anyone but Francie, and her face was white, but, "Hi, Francie," she said, and I was amazed to hear her voice sound as calm and friendly as if she was walking into Francie's room alone.

I swallowed hard, admiring her.

"Hi, Marie. Hi, Zadora. Why don't you push Francie over here by me where she can't run over the little kids."

Delores Benjamin's eyes were big and round. "Could she run over me?" she asked in a worried little voice. "Don't she have any brakes on that thing?"

I heard Irene Lord giggle nervously. Francie began to nod vigorously, and Delores inched closer. Then Marie bent down to show Delores how to keep the chair from rolling. "Sure, there's brakes," she said. "Look here, honey."

"I want a ride," the littlest Dooley girl, Joycie, yelled. "I want a ride!"

Delores whirled around, no longer interested in the brake. "Me too!" she cried. "Me too, me too." She began to dance up and down excitedly, while Joycie insisted, "I asked first. I asked first."

The other girls were beginning to laugh. Zadora smiled a little shakily. Marie looked up at Zadora, and Zadora shrugged. "I guess it's OK," she said.

"If . . ." said Marguerite firmly, surprising me again. She stepped forward and looked hard at them. "If it's OK with Francie. After all, it's *her* chair." But Francie was already leaning forward, holding her arms out to Marguerite.

Marguerite nodded. "Jeannie," she said. "Pile up some pillows over there to prop her with. Marie, can you help?" And in "two shakes of a lamb's tail," as Mother always said, Francie was pillowed in a place of honor on the bed, and Joycie had climbed into the wheelchair and was demanding, "Push me! Push me!"

16

Francie and the Kids

ZADORA SHOWED Alice Jane how to maneuver the wheel-chair over the edge of the rug, and Alice Jane pushed her little sister out into the hall where there was more room for a ride. The other girls crowded to the doorway to watch, all but Louise, who came back to the bed where Marguerite and I sat with Francie.

"That was kinda nice of her," Louise muttered, jerking her head toward Francie, but not looking at her. "Looked like she knew what the kids wanted to do and sorta said OK."

"Of course she knew," said Marguerite. "Honestly, Louise Dooley, just because you can't understand Francie doesn't mean she can't understand you!"

Francie's head was nodding, and she started to slip sideways, so I had to put my arm around her to prop her up. She grinned happily up at me, and I kept my arm around her and gave her a little squeeze.

"Uh . . . yeah . . ." said Louise. "Yeah, I guess not."

"If you listen hard," I said, "you might even be able

to understand her."

"Prih-dee," said Francie, reaching out to touch Louise's ruffled skirt. She fell forward, and Marguerite and I caught her just in time to keep her from sliding off the bed.

"Come closer, Louise," said Marguerite. "She wants to touch your dress. She likes to feel nice things."

"Prih-dee," said Francie.

Louise sat gingerly on the edge of the bed, looking sideways at Francie.

Francie happily patted the crisp pink ruffles that were now within her reach. "Prih-dee, prih-dee," she said.

"What's she saying?" said Louise.

"Listen," said Marguerite.

"Prih-dee, prih-dee," said Francie.

Louise tilted her head and looked straight at Francie for the first time.

"Pretty?" she said. "Is she saying 'pretty'?"

"Hey," I said. "You're good. It took me months to understand."

Louise blushed pink between her freckles. "Kinda like baby talk," she said. "We get lots of practice in our family with baby talk."

"Whatcha doing?" said Carol Lord. She had edged up to the bed, staring at us curiously.

"Hey," said Louise. "Didja know Francie can sorta talk?"

"Unh, unh," said Carol.

It was the funniest thing, and I still don't know exactly how it happened, but it wasn't ten minutes before all the girls were crowded around Francie and Marguerite and me on the bed, all but Delores, who was being pushed up and down the hall in the wheelchair by Marie. Suddenly, everyone was laughing and talking just like before the Hanisians came, only Francie was right in the middle of it all, jouncing a little on the bed, her hair slipping out of the blue bow, her blue eyes shining, happy and bright. And Marguerite was no longer ignored in the corner. She was busy translating Francie's garbled speech and showing the girls how to help Francie sit up or move. For the first time in a long time, she was acting like the popular sister I remembered from Oregon.

"That Marguerite Sloan isn't as stuck-up as I thought," I heard Louise whisper to Alice Jane as we went in to supper, and I was so surprised I didn't even get mad. Stuck-up? Is that what the kids had thought about Marguerite?

I don't suppose I ever ate so much in all my life as I ate that Christmas Eve at our neighborhood party, and that's saying something, because I love to eat—not like Marguerite, whose stomach turns at every little thing. But that night, even Marguerite got stuffed. We had all the usual holiday food—roast chicken and ham and mashed potatoes and pumpkin pie—and a whole lot of things I had never seen before, much less tasted. I tried them all. Mr. Benjamin was right. A person really hadn't lived until she had tasted Mrs. Benjamin's potato pancakes with sour cream.

"Sour cream?" said Eddie Dooley, making a face, but later I noticed him trying a taste from Alexander's plate; and he ended up eating all of Alexander's and going back for more.

Marguerite was disappointed to find she didn't much care for plum pudding, even if it was right out of Dickens. "Too much like fruitcake," she said, but she loved the dainty sugar-powdered cookies Mrs. Sisson said were made from her Swedish grandmother's recipe. I liked Mrs. Sisson's cookies too, and the small round loaves of bread Mrs. Hanisian called "pita" from Armenia, and Mrs. Lord's great, fluffy frosted lemon cake just like her mother used to make "down home in Lou'siana."

The grown-ups ate, sitting on the sofa and all the chairs we had, and Mr. Mendenhall and Warren ran next door for more because there weren't enough. They balanced their plates on their laps, and the mothers kept jumping up to run out to the kitchen to see if the coffee had finished perking or the punchbowl needed a refill or to bring in another boat of hot gravy. The fathers kept an eye on the boys to see that they didn't get too rambunctious; and I saw Mr. Sisson, whose children were all grown up, holding Gerald Dooley on his lap and feeding him bread and butter and chicken as fast as he could eat.

Us kids got to sit on the floor, just like at a picnic—all but Francie. Marguerite wheeled her over close to where we gathered in a cleared space in the dining room and stood by her chair to help her eat so there wouldn't be too much mess. The boys sat together and looked a little uneasy at first to see her there, but it wasn't long before they had stopped paying her any attention. There was too much to eat and too many things were happening all at once. The girls clustered around Francie's chair, as if they had always been around her. The bigger girls darted glances across at Alexander and Sammy, and I saw Marguerite giggle and whisper with them behind their hands, in the dumb way big girls do sometimes. The little kids kept jumping up and running in to their mothers to get their meat cut or beg for dessert. I saw Joycie Dooley sneak up behind Francie's chair and reach around when she thought no one was looking to put a gingerbread man on Francie's tray.

17

The Gift

IT WAS pretty late by the time we kids had carried all the plates and silver to the kitchen and the mothers had washed and dried and put them away. One by one, the little kids—Gerald and Joycie Dooley and Delores Benjamin—had fallen asleep, curled in some grown-up's lap, and been carried in to be tucked into Mother's and Daddy's big bed.

"Poor lambs, they'll miss opening their presents," said Mother.

"Sure, and they won't know the diff'rence," said Mrs. Dooley. "They can have them in the mornin', along with Santy Claus."

"Is it time?" I asked, eyeing the pile of gifts that had grown beneath the tree as our guests had arrived. I had put Alice Jane's jacks there early in the evening, along with Mother's and Daddy's packages, but I hadn't seen Marguerite put Sammy's sheet music under the tree. I hoped she hadn't forgotten. "Is it time?" I asked, feeling a little thrill of anticipation.

Mother caught Daddy's eye and nodded significantly.

He looked puzzled for a moment, then smiled as he understood. He held up his hands.

"Neighbors," he said in his big, deep voice. "Neighbors. Friends!"

Little by little, voices quieted and faded away. Mrs. Timothy and Zadora finished up in the kitchen and hurried through the swinging door to find places in the living room. Mr. Sisson tiptoed in from the bedroom, where he had been putting Gerald Dooley to bed. Sammy and Lloyd stopped tusseling behind the sofa and sat up expectantly. Marie Hanisian put the finishing touches on Louise Dooley's red hair, which she had been arranging in French braids. And Eddie Dooley scooted over to sit right at Daddy's feet, looking up at him. Everyone was still.

"Friends," said Daddy, looking around the crowded room. He smiled again, and his voice quieted. "Dear friends, thank you for coming to the first annual Stanley Avenue Christmas Eve Party."

There was a burst of applause, and Warren Mendenhall so far forgot himself as to cheer. When everyone laughed, he blushed pink and ducked his head, pulling off his spectacles and wiping them on his sleeve.

Mr. Lord heaved himself to his feet and waited until the room was quiet again.

"I think I speak for all the neighborhood," he said, "when I say, 'thank you,' to the Sloans for their hospitality. This evenin' has brought us all into a community of friendship. I don't think any of us will ever feel far from home ag'in.''

Once more our neighbors were clapping, smiling, and nodding at one another. I saw Mrs. Mendenhall reach out to squeeze her husband's hand; and as the applause died away, I could hear Francie's excited gurgling, but no one turned to stare, and only Mrs. Lord and Mrs. Timothy looked down at their laps with uncomfortable faces.

"And now," Daddy said, "it's time for the presents. Eddie, will you help me pass them out?"

Eddie sprang to his feet, puffing his chest out importantly, and followed Daddy to the tree, picking his way over and around the people who crowded our tiny living room.

One by one, Daddy drew packages from under the tree and read aloud the names of the recipients. "Irene. Mr. Benjamin. Alice Jane." When my name was called, Eddie brought me a package wrapped in silver gilt and tied with a silver cord. It contained a tiny crystal bottle, my first cologne. "To Jeanne, with love from Zadora," said the card. It smelled just like Zadora, beautiful and grownup, and I held it carefully in my hand, so it wouldn't break or spill.

Next to me, Sammy Benjamin was opening the present Marguerite had wrapped so carefully. She had not forgotten to put it under the tree, I thought. He drew out the sheet music, read the title of the piece and grinned. "Hey, swell," he said. He jumped to his feet, looking around for Marguerite; and when he saw her, standing beside Francie's chair, he marched straight up to her—or as straight as anyone could in that room stuffed with people—and stuck out his hand. "Gee, thanks," he said, gripping her hand in his and pumping it up and down. "How'd you know I wanted this? I've been telling Mrs. Sisson I could play it, but it's not in any of her books."

Marguerite looked shyly at the floor. "I could tell you were ready for it, listening to you practice," she said. "It's just something I'd like to play, if I knew how."

Mrs. Hanisian was sitting on a dining room chair, on the other side of Francie. She looked over at Marguerite sharply.

"Would you like to learn piano?" she said.

"We don't have a piano for practicing," said Marguerite.

"But you'd like to play?" said Mrs. Hanisian.

Marguerite shrugged, pressing her lips together hard.

"Well, say, Marguerite, thanks. This is swell," said Sammy.

"You're welcome, Sammy," said Marguerite.

Mrs. Hanisian looked at her thoughtfully.

"Now, here's an interesting one," said Daddy, who was still pulling packages from under the tree. The gift in his hand was wrapped just as Sammy's gift had been, in the bright holly-printed paper, with a sprig of holly tied on. "It says," said Daddy, "To Mamma." He looked around the room. "It seems to me there are several mammas here tonight," he said. Everyone laughed quietly. He peered at the tag again. "To Mamma from Francie," he read, and handed the package to Eddie and gave him a little push in Mrs. Hanisian's direction.

Mrs. Hanisian was looking puzzled. "From Francie?" she said, taking the package from Eddie's outstretched hand. She looked at Francie, and Francie grinned, bouncing in her chair the way she did when she was excited. Mrs. Hanisian began untying the string. People looked over curiously as she pulled the wrapping away to reveal a paper, rolled as Sammy's sheet music had been. Slowly she began to unroll the paper. I saw that Marguerite was gazing at her face as though hypnotized. Francie was jumping up and down, making louder and louder sounds.

"Fra-zhee made," she was yelling. "Fra-zhee made foh Mah-mah."

Mrs. Hanisian looked up from the paper she held unrolled in her beautiful, long-fingered hands. She looked about her dazed. "What in the world?" she said. "What . . ."

"Francie did it herself, Mrs. Hanisian," Marguerite said. "I helped her wrap it and wrote the tag, but Francie did the rest all by herself. She's been practicing every day with my paints. She wanted it to be a surprise."

Mrs. Hanisian looked at Marguerite as though she

didn't understand what she was saying. "Did it herself?" she said. She looked at Francie. "Francie, you did this yourself?"

Francie was making her strange, excited noises and bobbing her head as hard as she could. Her face was shining, and her eyes were so full of pride, I scarcely noticed she had begun to drool.

Mrs. Hanisian's eyes were filling with tears. "You taught her, didn't you, Marguerite?" she said, and Marguerite nodded.

"I knew she could do it. She can do things, if someone helps her find a way."

"What is it, my dear?" asked Mother.

"Yes, yes, what did Francie make?" everyone was asking.

Mrs. Hanisian slid from her chair to kneel beside Francie. She put an arm around her and whispered something into her ear. Then she turned and handed the paper to Marguerite. "Show everyone, Marguerite. Show everyone what Francie can do, when someone cares enough to teach her how." She undid Francie's straps and pulled her into her arms and sat on the floor, holding her tight while tears streamed down her cheeks.

The room had grown so still, I could hear the tick of the clock's pendulum as it swung back and forth. Marguerite unrolled the paper and turned it so everyone could see. "It's just that Francie wanted to learn to read and write like the rest of us kids," she said, her voice trembling, "so I've been teaching her how. That's all."

Blotched and wavery, the crooked black letters painted on the paper were large enough for everyone to read.

"Francie loves Mamma," they said.

18

Circle of Giving

I COULDN'T understand why everyone had gotten so quiet. A big smile spread over my face as I realized Marguerite had found a way to teach Francie to write. I didn't know whom I was prouder of—Francie or Marguerite.

The silence was broken by a sob. I looked, startled, to see who, besides Mrs. Hanisian, was crying. Mrs. Lord had put her round, pink face into her chubby hands and was weeping noisily, her ample shoulders heaving with her sobs. I glanced around then at the faces of our neighbors and friends. Mrs. Timothy's long nose had reddened at the tip, and her mouth was twisted in a crooked line. I saw Mr. Benjamin pull a huge white handkerchief from his pocket and blow his nose. Mrs. Mendenhall began to cluck her tongue and shake her head. The kids all looked puzzled, or uncomfortable. I felt my smile droop into a questioning frown, and I looked at Daddy for some clue as to what was wrong with everybody.

Daddy must have felt me looking at him, because his eyes met mine, and I saw his eyes were smiling even though his mouth was serious. He gave me a little nod, cleared his throat, and stepped over Eddie to put his arms around Marguerite. I saw his lips form the words, "I'm proud of you, sweetheart," when he hugged her, but I couldn't hear them because he was whispering in her ear.

Then, at last, I began to see the faces about me lighting up with smiles. Mrs. Lord began to mop her face with a ridiculously tiny lace-trimmed handkerchief.

"I declare," said Mrs. Sisson.

"Don't that beat all?" said Mr. Lord.

"I never would have thought . . ." said Mrs. Timothy.

Marguerite's face was bright red. She wriggled out of Daddy's arms and handed Francie's paper to Mrs. Hanisian. "Excuse me," she said in a choky voice and fled from the living room.

I saw Mother get up to follow and then sit down again when Daddy shook his head.

"Eddie," said Daddy, "there are still quite a few presents under this tree. You and I had better get busy."

By the time Daddy called Marguerite's name, she had slipped back into the living room. Her face still looked pink, and her eyes were bright. I could tell she hoped no one would notice her, but Francie saw her and began to holler, "Mahg! Mahg!" and so Marguerite made her way to where Mrs. Hanisian was still sitting on the floor and knelt beside them and let Francie help rip the paper off the package Eddie brought to her. It was an Irish linen handkerchief from Alexander Dooley. In fact, all the

Dooleys had given handkerchiefs, so quite a few people received them. "And a good thing too," said Daddy later, "with all the tears that flowed that night."

"It was the tears that brought us all together," Mother said, and later, thinking back on it, I knew she was right. More than the party, more than Christmas, more than anything, it was the tears and what they taught us about each other . . . the tears and the gifts. Oh, I don't mean the handkerchiefs and the cologne and the toys. I don't even mean Francie's gift to her mother, though maybe that comes closer. What I mean is how we learned the people in our neighborhood were a lot like the presents under our tree—some of the plainest and homeliest ones containing treasures, and some of the prettiest, shiniest ones holding only ordinary gifts. It was hard to tell from the wrappings just what was inside. It had been as hard to realize that Francie and her family, who looked so different, *felt* just like everyone else, as it had been to understand that the other neighborhood families, who seemed so much alike, each had special, individual qualities.

We began to learn about our neighbors that night we opened our home to them, and the learning went on and on: when Mrs. Dooley got sick the next spring and all the other mothers helped take care of her kids, and when Mrs. Timothy not only stopped talking about putting Francie in a home, but offered to watch her sometimes when Mrs. Hanisian went to the store, and when Mrs. Lord began to let Carol and Irene play with Francie, and oh so many other times in the coming years! For Marguerite, it was sharing Francie with the other kids that at last brought her friends of her own. The tears, and then these gifts, made us all friends.

I was sleepy when at last people began gathering up to leave. I remember the Dooleys trailing down the walk, lugging Gerald and Joycie wrapped in blankets. I saw Eddie stumble along holding Louise's hand, and his eyes kept going shut. Warren Mendenhall was trying to read the book someone had given him by the light of the porch lamp as his parents said goodnight, and Carol and Irene looked bleary-eyed and rumpled going down the steps in front of their mother and father.

I remember seeing Mrs. Benjamin help Mrs. Hanisian strap Francie into her chair. She was talking earnestly to Mrs. Hanisian, and we learned later she was offering to teach Francie. Before she and Mr. Benjamin were married, she had been a real schoolteacher. That was another of those gifts of self that began that night. From then on, Marguerite only helped teach Francie, for Mrs. Benjamin worked with her several times a week. "Francie needed a *real* teacher," Marguerite would say. "Besides, with Mrs. Benjamin teaching Francie, I have more time to practice."

Because that turned out to be one of the best things to come of the first annual Stanley Avenue Christmas Eve Party. Marguerite was given piano lessons at last.

"You gave Francie gifts of belief in her and faithfulness," Mrs. Hanisian told Marguerite that evening, when everyone else had gone home. "Francie passed those gifts to me by showing she can learn. I can make the circle of giving complete. From now on, for as long as you wish, our piano is yours to play whenever you like, and I will teach you."

I remember how Marguerite's face looked that night, all wondering and aglow.

"Lucky you," I said. "No more tap," and I was surprised to find I didn't feel the least bit jealous.

But Marguerite didn't hear. Not right then. She just walked to Mrs. Hanisian, her eyes wide and gray and dreaming, and did a strange thing—a courtly, romantic, old-fashioned sort of thing that somehow seemed just right. She took Mrs. Hanisian's beautiful hand in hers and bent her head over it and kissed it. And Mrs. Hanisian folded her in her arms. Francie grinned at them and chuckled deep in her throat, love shining from her big blue eyes. She shook her head back and forth, softly, softly.

It seems to me now, when I try to remember, that I heard Marguerite play the piano that Christmas Eve, but of course, that can't be right. It was late. I had curled up on the sofa, my head so heavy I had to lay it down against the maroon plush cushion. Mother and Marguerite stood at the door saying goodnight to the Hanisians, and Daddy went with them to help get Francie across the street.

I don't know why I seem to remember Marguerite's music that night. Perhaps it was Mrs. Hanisian I heard playing as I felt Daddy lift me from the sofa and carry me in to bed. It can't have been Marguerite after all. She had not yet learned to play, as she soon would, so her music told how she felt—sad or happy or wistful or mad. Yes, it must have been Mrs. Hanisian.

For I am certain I heard music ringing clear and joyous through the starry dark of that Christmas Eve.